MONSTERIOUS

TERROR IN
SHADOW CANYON

ALSO BY MATT MCMANN

Escape from Grimstone Manor
The Snatcher of Raven Hollow

MONSTERIOUS
TERROR IN SHADOW CANYON

MATT MCMANN

putnam

G. P. Putnam's Sons

G. P. PUTNAM'S SONS
An imprint of Penguin Random House LLC, New York

First published in the United States of America by G. P. Putnam's Sons,
an imprint of Penguin Random House LLC, 2023

Visit us online at PenguinRandomHouse.com.

Library of Congress Cataloging-in-Publication Data
Names: McMann, Matt, author.
Title: Terror in Shadow Canyon / Matt McMann.
Description: New York: G. P. Putnam's Sons, 2023. | Series: Monsterious ; [3] |
Summary: Twelve-year-old Tegan and his friends are stalked
by mysterious beasts while out on a weeklong wilderness backpacking trip.
Identifiers: LCCN 2023002421 (print) | LCCN 2023002422 (ebook) |
ISBN 9780593530757 (hardcover) | ISBN 9780593530771 (trade paperback) |
ISBN 9780593530764 (epub)
Subjects: CYAC: Monsters—Fiction. | Friendship—Fiction. |
Backpacking—Fiction. | Horror stories. | LCGFT: Horror fiction. | Novels.
Classification: LCC PZ7.1.M4636 Te 2023 (print) | LCC PZ7.1.M4636 (ebook) |
DDC [Fic]—dc23
LC record available at https://lccn.loc.gov/2023002421
LC ebook record available at https://lccn.loc.gov/2023002422

ISBN 9780593530757 (hardcover)
ISBN 9780593530771 (paperback)
1st Printing

Printed in the United States of America

LSCC

Design by Nicole Rheingans
Text set in Maxime Pro

To Michael Bourret, for a thousand and one reasons.

CHAPTER 1

"SEARCH TEAM, Bob here," the forest ranger said into his radio. "I've got something. Stand by."

He pushed back the brim of his hat as he knelt over a well-worn backpack. Propping it against a towering pine tree, he searched the various compartments. Compass. Swiss Army knife. Wool socks. First aid kit.

Tugging open a zipper on the inner lining, Bob removed a beat-up leather wallet. After examining the driver's license inside, he ran a rough hand over his stubbled beard, then stood and walked to a nearby cliff edge. A rapidly flowing river filled the canyon twenty-five feet below. With a deep sigh, he pulled the radio from his belt.

"Search team, Bob again. I found a backpack in sector four near the canyon edge. ID matches the missing hiker. Looks like we've got another cliff jumper."

"Roger that," crackled a voice from the radio. "Any sign of a body?"

"Negative," Bob said. "The rapids would have swept him downstream."

"Copy that. We'll send a team to check the area at first light. Good work, Bob. Come on back to base."

"Roger that. Bob out."

He hoisted the pack onto his shoulder with a shake of his head. This was the third hiker to go missing in his section of Shadow Canyon this year.

Why couldn't these thrill seekers get their kicks somewhere else? While logic told him they were all tragic accidents, it was hard to forget the rumors that this forest was haunted.

The sun slid behind a nearby mountain peak, spreading shadows through the deepening twilight. As he did a final visual sweep of the area, Bob noticed an unusual root structure on the exposed base of a fallen oak. The vertical roots spread wide in an oddly symmetrical pattern, like the limbs of a giant crab. He shivered in the gloom.

"Get a grip," Bob muttered, trying to shove the spooky stories from his mind. "You're a forest ranger, for goodness' sake."

He turned and walked quickly through the trees toward base camp.

As he hurried away, one of the strangely shaped roots began to move, waving eerily in the gathering night.

CHAPTER 2

"I'VE NEVER seen so many different ways to die," Tegan said.

He stood beside his best friends Marcus and Ning at the edge of the parking lot near the Shadow Canyon trailhead. Ning's mom had planned this hiking trip to celebrate their sixth grade graduation. Tegan's mom was supposed to be here, but at the last minute she had to work, and his dad came instead. She said it would be a good bonding experience for them. Tegan wasn't so sure. He eyed his dad warily, waiting for him to do something embarrassing. Again.

The three friends, along with Tegan's dad and Ning's mom, stared at a large warning sign covered with graphics of stick figures in distress.

"I like the cliff jumper," Ning said, resting her chin on her walking stick. "I give him a nine for style."

"They do look entertaining," Yanay said, peering around her daughter's shoulder. "But it's no joke. People have died messing around in this canyon."

"And people have died on merry-go-rounds," said Ed, Tegan's dad. "Sheesh, lighten up, Yanay. We're here to have fun, remember?"

Tegan looked at his hiking boots, his face flushed. He wished his dad had just stayed home with Milo, his *favorite* son. Ever since Tegan's little brother was born seven years ago, Ed had given Milo most of his attention. Tegan felt like he'd been replaced.

Yanay took a calming breath. "Learning the dangers before going into rugged terrain helps things *stay* fun. Besides, did you notice the venomous spiders warning?" She couldn't quite hide her smirk as she pointed to the sign's photos of a black widow and a yellow sac spider.

Ed's pale skin grew a shade lighter. "I hate spiders."

Marcus pushed up his glasses and inched his stocky frame closer to the sign. "Hidden rocks, undertow, hydraulic suction . . . I'm surprised there's not a shark warning."

"Mountain river sharks," Ning said, squinting in the bright morning sun. "Definitely have to watch out for those."

Tegan picked up his pack with a groan. Ning, an experienced hiker, had helped her mom organize their supplies and distribute the weight based on each person's size. With her tall frame and muscular build, Ning was carrying more than Tegan, but his pack still felt heavy, and they hadn't even started hiking yet. *How am I going to lug this through the wilderness for a week?* he thought gloomily.

Noticing his expression, Yanay smiled. "Hang in there, Tegan. You'll get stronger as we go, and your pack will lighten as we eat the food."

Marcus snugged his baseball cap over his box braids and looked eagerly down the trail. This outing was one big field trip to him. He planned on collecting nature samples for their seventh grade science fair that fall.

Tegan rubbed sunscreen on his pale nose and joined Ning at the trailhead.

"Here's hoping we don't die," she said, her dark eyes flashing beneath her straight black bangs.

Tegan laughed nervously. Hiking wasn't really

his thing. He stared at the brooding forest, trying to convince himself there was nothing to be afraid of.

He couldn't shake the feeling that something was staring back.

CHAPTER 3

THEY HIKED along a meandering trail through tall evergreens. Sunbeams painted golden splotches on the ground. Birds chirped, squirrels scampered from tree to tree, and everything was lush and green. The air felt crisp and smelled of pine needles. Surprising himself, Tegan was glad he'd let Ning talk him into the trip.

Then he saw the suspension bridge over the ravine.

Marcus ran up to the yawning chasm and looked down. "Whoa, check this out!"

"Not too close to the edge," Yanay warned. "Welcome to Shadow Canyon."

At the bottom of the ravine ran a fast-moving river dotted with rapids. Rocky outcroppings on the canyon walls threw dark shadows over the water. The only way across was a narrow suspension bridge, swaying slightly in the wind.

"I am *not* going on that thing," Tegan said.

"Oh, come on, T, it's fine," his dad said. "Watch." Ed walked to the middle of the bridge and jumped up and down, tugging at the waist-high cables on either side. The bridge bucked and swayed ominously.

"Cut it out, Dad," Tegan said. "I get the point."

Ed laughed and walked to the far side.

Marcus examined the end of the bridge. "These cables are wound for extra strength and anchored in the rock." He flashed Tegan a reassuring smile. "Nothing to worry about."

Ning nudged Tegan. "Besides, if you do fall, you won't have long to think about it."

"Thanks, I feel much better now," he said as his friends headed onto the bridge.

Yanay came up beside him. "A bridge like this can be a little freaky when you're not used to it. Why don't we cross together? I'll stay right behind you."

Tegan nodded reluctantly and edged out onto the wooden planks. The bridge swayed slightly, and he could feel the vibration of Ning's footsteps. He glanced down at the river, and his head swam.

"Take deep breaths and keep your eyes on the far side," Yanay said in a calm voice. "You've got this."

Clutching the main cables tightly with both hands, Tegan inched his way across. He clenched his jaws and moved toward Marcus and Ning, who called out encouragements from the far side. Already across, Ed continued along the trail and disappeared. Watching him go, Tegan's heart dropped. His mom would *never* do that.

Finally, Tegan stepped onto wonderfully solid ground as his friends and Yanay cheered.

"Good job," Ning said. "Now you've got a whole week until you have to do it again."

CHAPTER 4

SECLUDED FAR from the hated sunshine, the creature shifted her massive bulk and gazed over her sleeping children. Her joints ached from the weight of many years. As she stretched one long leg, her claws brushed the remnants of her last meal, sending a hiking boot tumbling from her rocky throne.

With a wheezing sigh, she blinked her many eyes and settled down to wait. Hopefully, the hunt would be successful tonight.

She was hungry again.

CHAPTER 5

"LOOK AT the size of that thing!" Marcus exclaimed.

In a meadow near the trail, a huge oval rock lay like a fallen monolith. Tegan's eyebrows lifted. "That is one big rock." He looked for others as they continued hiking but didn't see any.

A few hours later, they stopped for lunch in a clearing high above the river. Ed dropped his backpack and, after pulling off his hiking boots, started unbuckling his pants.

"Dad!" Tegan exclaimed in horror. "What are you doing?"

"Relax," Ed said. "I've got my swimsuit on under these. Nothing like a dip in a mountain river. Who's with me?"

"You're joking, right, Mr. Campbell?" Ning said as she looked over the edge. "There's no path down to the water."

"Don't need a path when you jump."

"That's at least a twenty-foot drop," Tegan said. "And there could be underwater rocks."

"Twenty feet is nothing," Ed said dismissively. "Back in college, I used to jump thirty feet into a river off a railway bridge."

Marcus's forehead wrinkled in concern. "But the warning sign at the trailhead said not to cliff jump."

"The park department has to put those signs up

to keep from getting sued." Ed continued to undress. "I'm a good swimmer. And you can tell the deep parts by the color of the water."

"Listen to the kids, Ed," Yanay said. "You're being reckless."

"And as usual, you're being too cautious. Everyone should be a little reckless sometimes. Makes you feel alive." Ed walked to the edge and peered down. "Look! A perfect calm spot, nice and deep. Sure nobody else wants to go?"

"Please don't," Tegan said. "I mean, how are you gonna get back up here?"

"Climb," he said, pointing down at the cliff. "There are plenty of handholds." He backed up to get a running start. "Here we go!"

Ed raced to the edge and launched himself into space. Everyone heard the splash as they rushed forward and peered down anxiously. The ripples were already being swept away by the current, but there was no sign of Tegan's father.

"Come on, Ed," Yanay muttered.

Tegan's stomach clenched as the seconds dripped by. What if his dad didn't come up? What would they do? How could he tell his mom?

"Why do you all look so nervous?" asked a voice ringing up from below.

Ed's grinning head hovered above the water in the shadow of the opposite canyon wall.

"Dad!" Tegan called out, his relief mixed with anger. "What are you doing way over there?"

"I swam underwater to throw you off. Just having a little fun. You should have seen your faces!"

"Fun? You really freaked us out."

Yanay gave an exasperated sigh. "Seriously, Ed. Not amusing."

"Okay, okay, I'm sorry. I'm coming out."

Yanay walked away shaking her head.

Ed swam across the river until he reached the cliff wall below them. "I think I see a good sp—" He suddenly disappeared beneath the water.

Tegan groaned. "He really doesn't know when to give up."

"Maybe a river shark got him," Ning said with a smirk.

"Uh, hold up . . ." Marcus said, a frown creasing his dark brown skin. "I think something might really be wrong this time."

Tegan snorted. "Nah, he's just goofing—"

Ed broke the surface, his arms flailing. "Help!" he cried before being yanked under.

"Dad!" Tegan yelled.

Yanay ran over. "I'm going down!"

Ning grabbed her arm. "I've got it." She clambered over the edge of the cliff.

"Ning, wait!"

"It's okay," Marcus said. "She's the best rock climber in school."

"But what can she do?" Tegan said, gripping his thick blond hair with both hands. "What's happening to him?"

Marcus's eyes widened. "Hydraulic suction! It was on the warning sign. Underwater vortexes can form near the canyon walls, even when it looks calm on the surface. They're strong enough to pull swimmers under!"

Yanay called down to Ning. "Stay out of the water!" She put a hand to her forehead, then turned to Tegan and Marcus. "We need a strong stick, as long as you can find. Go!"

They scattered, frantically searching the surrounding forest. Tegan tripped and banged his knee on a rock. Tears of frustration filled his eyes as panic shot through him. *My dad is drowning*, he thought. He spotted a long stick poking up through a carpet of pine needles. Yanking it free, Tegan raced back to the cliff edge.

Yanay snatched the stick from his hand. Throwing herself onto her stomach, she leaned over the edge of the ravine. "Ning! Catch!"

Ning was balancing precariously on a rock ledge near the water. She caught the stick and thrust it into the river. Tegan watched, horrified, as she swirled it around while leaning dangerously forward. How long had it been since his dad had surfaced? Could he already be dead?

Ning gave a cry and hauled back on the stick, grunting with effort. A moment later, Ed's hand broke the surface, clutching the stick, followed by his head. Ning towed him to the ledge, where he clung, coughing and choking.

CHAPTER 6

"I'M SORRY," Ed said as he dried off beside the trail. "I promise I'll be more careful."

Tegan rubbed the tear tracks from his smudged face. He loved his dad, but Ed rarely stopped to think of how his actions might affect other people. Even his own son. Sometimes Tegan wondered which of them was twelve and which was forty.

"No more almost dying, okay?" Yanay said.

"Scout's honor," Ed said, holding up his hand in a failed attempt at the Boy Scout salute.

"Your dad's really something," Marcus muttered to Tegan, rolling his eyes.

A sour feeling rose in Tegan's stomach. "If my mom had come like she was supposed to, we wouldn't have to deal with him."

After a subdued lunch, they continued hiking. Marcus enthusiastically shared nature facts: Coast Douglas firs grow up to two hundred and fifty feet. Woodpeckers drum on trees for insects and to establish their territory. Local predators included black bears, mountain lions, and timber wolves. Tegan wasn't thrilled with that one.

An hour later, Yanay called out, "Here it is!" She pointed to a small orange tag nailed to a tree beside the trail. It was marked with the letters *EF*.

"Is this the trail to Emerald Falls?" asked Tegan.

"Sort of," Ning said. "These are the trail signs that mark the beginning of the cross-country route."

"The pictures of Emerald Falls I found online

were amazing!" Marcus said. "But it's really hard to reach. Not many people hike that far."

"It's definitely off the beaten path," Yanay said. "Actually, there is no path."

"How do we find the falls?" Tegan asked. "Follow the tags?"

"Yep," Ning said. She scanned the surrounding trees and pointed to one about forty feet away. "You see the next orange tag? Each one is placed within sight of the last. Follow them, and they lead to Emerald Falls."

"Like Hansel and Gretel's bread crumbs," Marcus said.

"Didn't they end up lost in the woods after birds ate the crumbs?" Tegan asked.

Ed chuckled. "Good thing birds don't eat orange tags."

They left the trail and headed into the raw wilderness. Hiking became much more difficult as they wound their way around rocky outcroppings, climbed over fallen trees, and wriggled through thick brush, always following the elusive orange tags. Most were easy to spot, but occasionally new growth forced them to hunt for the next one. The tags zigzagged randomly to mark out a manageable route, and Tegan quickly lost all sense of direction.

The scenery was beautiful: towering, shaggy-barked pines dripping moss. Rugged mountain peaks. Gurgling streams with quiet pools. Colorful wildflowers. Tegan even noticed unexpected things like a smooth football-sized stone embedded in the dirt between tree roots.

After four hours with not many breaks, Tegan's feet felt as if they were strapped to bowling balls. He plopped onto a log. "I'm . . . done," he said, gasping for breath.

Yanay glanced around. "Actually, this is a good place to camp."

With Yanay directing, they put up their tents, then collected rocks and wood for a firepit. Ning started the campfire, and they roasted hot dogs and made s'mores. As darkness fell, Ed entertained them with spooky stories in the flickering firelight. After nodding off, Tegan jerked his head up to hear his dad finish a tale.

"Enjoy your snooze?" Ed asked.

Yanay gave a loud yawn. "I think Tegan's got the right idea. Let's douse the fire and go to bed."

"Can't we leave the fire going?" Tegan asked anxiously. Other than the moon and stars, it was pitch-black, and the surrounding forest had a menacing quality.

Ning shook her head. "Forest fire risk. As dry as it's been, this place could go up fast." After smothering the fire with dirt, she pulled a long rope from her pack. "Just need to hang the food bags."

"Why?"

"Keeps them from bears."

Tegan's eyes widened. "I'm not tired anymore."

With the bags secured, they said good night. Ed had his own tent, while Ning bunked with her mom, and Tegan shared with Marcus. As they crawled into their sleeping bags, Marcus mumbled sleepily, "This is the best trip ever."

Soon, Marcus was snoring gently. Tegan wriggled in his sleeping bag, trying to find a spot free of roots or stones. He finally drifted into a troubled sleep, dreaming of bears ripping through the thin nylon tent.

From the shadows beneath the trees, a different predator silently watched the sleeping camp, one far stranger than a bear.

And far more deadly.

CHAPTER 7

"WHAT DO you mean, 'gone'?" Ning asked the next morning. She and the others sat near their tents finishing a cold breakfast of protein bars and fruit.

"I mean I can't find the next orange marker," Yanay said, her tan skin flushed with frustration. She'd just returned from scouting ahead. "I could have sworn I saw it yesterday."

"We'll help," Marcus said.

"Thanks. Stay in sight of each other and the camp."

They split up and searched the surrounding trees. As the minutes slipped by without the next marker being found, anxious thoughts began swirling in Tegan's mind. There was nothing but endless forest in every direction.

They gathered back at the campsite. Marcus looked glum.

"All my research showed the route was intact," Yanay said. "I don't understand why it would stop partway like this." Her tension spread to the others as she muttered, "I *know* I saw the next marker."

"Can we find Emerald Falls without the tags?" Marcus asked.

Yanay shook her head. "Not with all the switchbacks in this rugged terrain. We could get lost, and there's no cell service. That's too risky this far from a maintained trail."

"So we have to go back?" Ning asked.

"I think that's our only choice," Yanay said. "There's other cool stuff to see in this area besides Emerald Falls. I'm really sorry."

"That's okay," Tegan said. "We'll have fun anyway." Though secretly relieved to abandon the grueling hike, he knew the others were disappointed. He wished he could help, but he was the least outdoorsy of the group. The only nature experience he'd had was a week of archery camp last summer.

"It's all good, Mom," Ning said.

Marcus nodded in agreement, but Ed just shook his head and walked away. Yanay glared at him before turning to pack up her tent.

"Are you doing okay with your dad being here?" Ning asked Tegan quietly.

He glanced down and scraped the heel of his boot in the dirt. "I really wish my mom had come like we planned."

"My mom wasn't too happy about the switch either," Ning said. "She was really looking forward to spending time with Jenny."

"So your mom stayed back to work and watch Milo?" Marcus asked.

Tegan nodded glumly. He'd never really clicked with his dad the way his younger brother did, and while Ed made a point to spend time with Milo, he only hung out with Tegan when they did something as a whole family. For Tegan's last birthday, he'd had a few friends over to the house, and his dad sat around looking bored while his mom grilled burgers. But when Milo's birthday came, Ed rented Trampoline City for Milo and ten friends, and it was hard to tell which of them was having more fun. Tegan knew Milo was outgoing like Ed, and they had more in common, but that didn't make his dad's lack of effort with him hurt any less.

After they'd packed, Yanay led them back the

way they'd come. A minute later, she stopped and looked around carefully.

"Do you see something, Mrs. Chen?" Marcus asked.

"No," she said. "That's the problem. I can't find the last tag we passed yesterday."

The group spread out and began scanning the trees. After ten minutes of fruitless searching, they came back together.

"I don't understand it," Yanay said. "How is this possible?"

The trail markers behind them had also disappeared.

CHAPTER 8

"BUT THEY were there yesterday," Marcus said in disbelief.

"Looks like someone ate our bread crumbs after all," Ning said. "Or some*thing*."

"This trip is getting better all the time," Ed said darkly.

Tegan wrung his hands, trying not to panic. "But we can still get back to the main trail, right?"

"I'll admit, it'll be challenging," Yanay said. "It

was a really winding route to get here. But with my compass, we should be fine."

Tegan sighed with relief as Yanay dug a compass from her pack. Then he noticed her forehead furrow. "Everything okay?"

"It's my compass," Yanay said. "It's going berserk."

They all crowded around her. Instead of steadily pointing north, the compass needle swung wildly.

"What's wrong with it?" Ning asked.

"I have no idea," Yanay said.

Marcus scanned the surrounding rocks. "I read in a nature forum that iron ore in rocky areas can throw off a compass."

"They used to mine iron around here back in the sixties," Ed said. Everyone looked at him in surprise. "Hey, I read sometimes too. I researched Shadow Canyon before the trip."

"I have a backup map," Yanay said, pulling a waterproof sheet from her pack and holding it out. To Tegan, it was a confusing mass of letters, numbers, and squiggly lines.

"So where are we on here, Mom?" Ning asked, peering over Yanay's shoulder.

Yanay didn't answer as she studied the map, looked at the surrounding terrain, then back at the map. Finally, she sighed. "Honestly, I have no idea. I was never the best at reading topography maps, and this area is so filled with peaks and streams and winding ravines that I can't tell which landmark is which."

"So now we have no compass and a map we can't read?" Tegan asked, his voice rising in pitch. "How are we gonna get back?"

"Relax, Tegan," Ed said. "We're gonna be fine. Right, Yanay?"

She forced a smile. "Of course. We'll figure it out."

"Can't we just walk back toward the main trail?" Ning said, pointing. "It's that way, so we'll hit it eventually."

Yanay looked grim. "That might seem like the right direction, but the route coming here twisted so much, I don't think any of us can be certain."

"The sun!" Tegan blurted out. "Don't people navigate by the sun?"

"That will help, but sun navigation is only for large-scale, general directions," Yanay said. "And the heavy clouds and thick trees won't help."

"So what do we do?" Ning asked, a tremor in her voice.

They all looked at Yanay. She hesitated. "To be honest, I'm torn. We can try to find our way back to the main trail, or we can wait here. I filed our trip with the ranger station. If we're not back on time, they'll send someone to look for us."

"But how will they find us without the orange tags?" Marcus asked. "*They* won't have a route to follow either."

Yanay looked uncomfortable. "That's true."

Ed sighed. "I guess we hunt for the main trail." He gestured toward Yanay. "After you, boss."

CHAPTER 9

THE MOUNTAIN lion looked up sharply as the wind shifted. Peering through the trees with her large round eyes, she spied a clearing. Raising her muzzle, she sniffed, testing the air.

A low growl rumbled in her tawny chest, but she wasn't angry—she was afraid. Turning, the mountain lion sprinted silently in the opposite direction.

The clouds shifted and sunlight fell across a cliff face on the far side of the clearing, revealing the yawning black entrance to a cave.

Seeping from the cave was the metallic scent of blood.

CHAPTER 10

THE NEXT few hours were tense.

The group hiked mostly in silence, eyes peeled for orange tags that never appeared. The weather turned gloomy, with heavy clouds sweeping overhead like ships in a gale. Yanay climbed a rocky ridge and scanned the horizon. Tegan clambered up beside her, and they stood quietly for a few moments.

"We're lost, huh?" he said softly.

Yanay stared at him as if she was trying to read something in his eyes. "Not completely. Shadow

Canyon is south of us, so I'm trying to head that direction using the sun. But we can't hike straight south because of the terrain, and with the way the river twists, we could approach at a spot where it bends away from us. I climbed up here hoping to see a gap in the trees that showed the canyon's location."

Tegan gazed out at an endless forest broken only by rugged peaks and dark valleys. It felt like they were the only people on earth. His anxious thoughts whirled like leaves in a storm. Tears blurred his vision, and he wiped his nose on his sleeve.

Yanay put a hand on his shoulder. "You okay?"

Tegan almost told her the truth. That he was scared. That he missed his mom. That he wished his dad was someone he could confide in and go to for comfort. But Ed wasn't that kind of father—not even to Milo. Tegan had learned long ago that his dad didn't express his feelings or know how to respond to people who did. Even his wife and sons.

Tegan blinked away his tears. "Yeah. I'm okay." Before Yanay could see the lie on his face, he scrambled down to the others. Ed was telling a joke to Marcus and Ning, trying to lighten the mood. It wasn't working.

A few moments later, Yanay came back. "We just have to keep heading south as best we can." She squeezed Ning's shoulders, and they walked off arm in arm. Tegan stared after them with a new weight in his gut. He looked at his dad, who picked up his pack and followed the pair without a backward glance.

Tegan fell in behind them, swallowing a lump in his throat that had nothing to do with being lost.

CHAPTER 11

"MRS. CHEN, did you see this?" Marcus asked.

He was hunched over a smooth stone the size of a swollen football. It was wedged between the exposed roots of a huge pine tree, half buried in the dirt.

Yanay joined him. "That's odd."

"I saw one yesterday," Tegan said.

She rapped the stone with her knuckles, producing a dull thunk. "Must be a type of rock common to this area. But there's something unusual about the way it's tucked between these roots. It doesn't look quite natural."

"Maybe they're like the sliding rocks of Death Valley," Marcus said.

"And for those of us who aren't science geeks?" Ning asked.

"There's a flat area in Death Valley National Park where big stones mysteriously move, leaving tracks in the dirt as long as fifteen hundred feet," Marcus said. "Some of them weigh up to seven hundred pounds! Scientists have been studying them for years."

Yanay nodded. "I heard recently that the smaller rocks move when there's a rare combination of melting ice and wind."

"But that doesn't account for the big ones," Marcus said. "Still a mystery."

Ed smirked. "Maybe we'll be the ones to solve the mystery of the Shadow Canyon stones. Don't wet yourself, Tegan. I can hold your hand if things get too spooky for you."

Marcus frowned as Tegan's face flushed with a familiar mix of hurt and embarrassment.

"Real nice, Ed," Yanay said.

"I was kidding! The kids joke with each other all the time. What's the difference?"

Tegan snatched up his pack and pushed through the trees, quickly followed by Marcus, Ning, and Yanay. Sighing, Ed trudged after them with a gloomy expression.

As the day wore away beneath their tromping feet, Tegan became more discouraged. On top of the tension with his dad, the beautiful scenery was now lost on him. The endless sameness of the forest made it feel like they were walking in circles. Given how often they'd been forced to backtrack because of a ravine or a cliff, maybe they were.

Yanay checked her compass repeatedly as they

hiked, but it still wasn't functioning. When they reached a clearing that afternoon, she called for a break. Tegan flopped to the ground and gulped greedily from his canteen. With all the streams in the area, at least water wasn't a problem. Unfortunately, Yanay said they joined the Shadow River too far upstream to follow them to the trail.

Birdcalls and the scampering of small animals highlighted the group's silence. With everyone's mind on their increasingly bad situation, conversation had died out hours ago. Tegan chewed moodily on a strip of jerky.

Finally, Ning said, "That thing is creeping me out."

They followed her gaze to the base of a large fallen tree at the edge of the clearing. Its now vertical root structure had an oddly symmetrical shape. There were four long, bent roots on either side and two smaller roots sticking up from the top. A large bulbous clod of dirt filled out the bottom with a smaller clod on top, like the world's ugliest snow-man. Or in this case, rootman.

"It's just the bottom of a tree," Marcus said. "The roots only look strange because they're sticking up in the air instead of in the ground."

"I'm with Ning," Tegan said. "I noticed one like that earlier."

"The forest is a spooky place," Ed said.

"Don't encourage them," said Yanay. "We have enough on our hands without worrying about oddly shaped tree roots."

Much to the dislike of Tegan's aching feet, they resumed their search for the trail. Over the next few hours, they saw three more of the mysterious stones embedded between tree roots. Tegan and Ning played a game of who could spot the creepiest-looking root system on fallen trees.

As twilight fell, Yanay selected a level clearing for their campsite. Tegan dropped his pack and sank gratefully onto a log. Even Ning, the fittest of the group, looked wiped out.

"Tegan, why don't you and Marcus gather firewood while the rest of us set up the tents?" Yanay said. "Stay together and in sight of camp."

Tegan sighed wearily but nodded. Marcus pulled him to his feet, and they wandered off.

"How are you doing with all this?" Tegan asked when they were alone.

Marcus bent to pick up a large pine cone, then pushed up his glasses. "Um. Well, not great. I mean, it's really cool being out here and everything, but . . ." He placed the pine cone in his pocket, another sample for his science project.

"Yeah," Tegan said. "What really bugs me is what happened to the trail tags."

"I know, right?" Marcus said. "Who could have done that? And why?"

Tegan shrugged. "No clue. It's . . . creepy." He

glanced around uneasily at the rapidly darkening woods. Nightfall came on quickly in the mountains. Another mass of strangely shaped tree roots jutted up nearby, and Tegan shivered.

The boys' arms were loaded when they heard a scrambling sound. Tegan spied a chipmunk climbing a towering pine. It spiraled around the trunk in fits and starts. A moment later, a huge owl swooped in, flapping its wings as it tried to snatch the chipmunk with its hooked talons.

"Whoa!" Marcus said.

The chipmunk darted to safety among the thicker branches. The owl settled in a nearby tree, looking down imperiously, as if trying to appear dignified after failing to catch its dinner.

"That was awesome!" Marcus said, hurrying toward camp. "I've got to tell the others."

As Tegan took a last look at the owl, the sun sank behind a nearby peak, and the darkness thickened.

A hint of movement caught his eye. He glanced over at the creepy bunch of roots he'd seen earlier.

One of the outstretched roots moved, bending gently in the gloom.

"Impossible," Tegan whispered. He blinked hard and stared again. A second root began to move stiffly, like an old man stretching his leg. It must be the wind, Tegan told himself. Or a trick of the light.

Heart thumping, he turned and fled.

CHAPTER 12

"AND SWOOPING around the tree was a giant *owl*!" Marcus said as Tegan stumbled into camp. "It was so cool!"

Ning stared at Tegan. "What's up? You look like you saw a ghost."

He dumped his armload of wood and tried to catch his breath. "I . . . I saw . . ." What *did* he see, exactly?

"I know," his dad said, snapping his fingers. "It was Bigfoot, right?" He cupped his hands around his mouth and called, "Oh, Mr. *Foot*! Come on in, we'd love to meet ya!"

Tegan clenched his jaw. "Never mind."

Marcus cooked stew over the campfire by adding water to packets of dehydrated beef, powdered gravy, and seasonings. Tegan found it surprisingly tasty. Under the influence of the cheerfully crackling fire, he began to relax, listening to the murmur of conversation without feeling the need to join in.

When Marcus dropped down beside him, Tegan said, "That stew was really good. You should be a chef."

"Yeah, I'm great at adding water to stuff," Marcus said with a wry smile. He glanced around at the dark forest. "What I really want to do is this."

"Wander aimlessly through the woods?"

"Nature stuff," Marcus said. "Be a forest ranger maybe, or work with animals at a zoo."

"That sounds pretty cool."

Marcus frowned slightly. "Tell that to my parents. They want me to be an engineer or something, but that's just not me."

"Have you talked to them about it?"

"I've tried, but they think I'm only saying that because I'm a kid."

Tegan glanced over at his dad. "Yeah, parents can be tough to talk to sometimes."

The overcast skies cleared, and under a blanket of stars, Ed launched into one of his endless repertoire of spooky stories. This one was about blind sloth creatures with huge claws closing in on an unsuspecting group of campers. Ning was laughing, while Marcus leaned forward with his fists against his chest.

Ed lowered his voice dramatically. "And then from the deep, dark forest came an unearthly—"

A loud rustling from the shadows beneath the trees made him pause. Everyone looked toward the sound but saw nothing.

There was a heavy silence.

"Looks like they're here," Ed said ominously.

They all chuckled nervously. Tegan remembered the roots moving as if they were alive. That's ridiculous, he told himself. Tree roots *don't* move.

"As the campers slept," Ed continued, "the bloodthirsty monsters made their move. They approached the tents so slowly and quietly that the campers never knew they were there . . . until it was too late!"

"Too late?" Marcus whispered. "Wh-why too late?"

"Because the monsters reached out with their razor-sharp claws and—"

From out of the darkness, a creature stepped into the firelight.

CHAPTER 13

MARCUS SHRIEKED, and everyone jumped. It took a moment to realize that the fearsome intruder was . . .

A raccoon. A fluffy, roly-poly raccoon.

They all burst out laughing. Marcus ran a hand over his hair with a sheepish grin.

"Awww, look!" Ning cried.

Three baby raccoons came tumbling and bumbling along after their mother.

"They're adorable!" Tegan said.

The raccoon family ignored them as they snuffled around looking for food.

"Don't touch them," Yanay warned. "They're cute, but a mother raccoon protecting her young can be dangerous. And they could make a real mess of our supplies."

"Captain Cautious swoops in once again," Ed said, rolling his eyes. "I think we can take them."

Yanay glowered at him, but said nothing.

After the raccoons wandered off, Ning made hot chocolate. Tegan zipped up his hooded sweatshirt against the evening chill and leaned back against the twisted roots of a large tree. Half buried in the dirt beside him was another mysterious rock.

Yanay sighed. "I'm really sorry. I thought we'd have reached the trail by now."

"It's not your fault, Mom," Ning said. "You're doing great."

"Yeah, I bet we'll find it tomorrow," Marcus said.

"But to be safe, maybe Tegan should rub that stone for good luck." He nodded his head toward the rock.

Tegan smirked, but played along. He reached out and rubbed the rock's mottled gray surface. It felt warm, probably from absorbing the campfire's heat. As he leaned forward to take his mug from Ning, his sweatshirt held him back. He shifted, trying to free himself, but the shirt stuck fast.

"What's with this root?" Tegan asked, craning his neck to look behind him. He pulled again. "Let. Me. Go!"

"I'll get it," Marcus said, standing.

Then he froze, his gaze fixed over Tegan's head. His eyes swelled as he pointed, his hand trembling. Above Tegan in the deep shadows beside the tree, huge, glassy eyes shone in the firelight.

Eight of them.

Tegan yelped in fright and tried to leap away, but his sweatshirt yanked him back.

"What *is* that?" Ed said, his voice pitched high in fear.

"Help me!" Tegan cried.

Marcus stumbled over and tugged open the zipper on the front of Tegan's sweatshirt. Tegan lurched forward, sliding his arms free and leaving the pinned shirt behind. He plowed into Marcus, and they fell in a heap beside the fire.

Yanay leaped up, her face a mask of disbelief as Ed scrambled backward like a frightened crab. Ning snatched a burning stick from the flames and stepped forward, holding it toward the unblinking collection of eyes.

Instantly, they winked out and disappeared.

CHAPTER 14

"BUT WHAT *were* they?" Tegan asked, panic evident in his voice. The group huddled on the far side of the fire and glanced uneasily into the dark forest.

"There are plenty of animals in this area," Yanay said. "Many are nocturnal."

"But those eyes were *huge*!" Ning said.

"Some of the animals are big," Yanay replied, trying to remain calm. "Moose, elk, bears, mountain lions, wolves—"

"You are *not* making me feel better," Tegan said.

"Strange that there were four of them," Ed said. "Eight eyes all together like that means the animals must have been clumped pretty tight. Is that normal?"

"Well, no," Yanay said. "But wolves are pack animals. It could have been four wolves."

"I don't think so," Marcus said softly. Normally animated, he'd been unusually quiet during the discussion. They fell silent and looked at him. He lifted his gaze from the fire. "The eyes were in rows. Four on top of four."

"It must have been two smaller animals in front of two bigger ones," Yanay said.

Marcus shook his head. "The eyes moved together. Perfectly together. When Ning approached with the flaming branch, they didn't turn away one set at a time. They vanished all at once." He looked slowly at each of them. "Like they belonged to a single creature."

Tegan stared hard at Marcus, his dread growing. "But what kind of creature has eight eyes?"

Marcus took a deep breath. "A spider."

There was a long pause.

Then Ed burst out laughing, a little too loud. "Good one, Marcus! A spider. You tell better stories than I do." He shifted uneasily.

"But you saw how big those eyes were," Ning said, her voice strained. "And how high off the ground. It would have to be a spider the size of—"

"I know," Marcus cut in. "It sounds crazy and probably is. I'm just trying to come up with an answer that fits the facts."

Tegan shivered, more from their discussion than the chill night air. He hugged himself, rubbing his arms. He glanced over to where his sweatshirt lay, still hooked on a tree root.

"Um . . . somebody wanna come with me to get my shirt?"

When his dad didn't move, Yanay stood, and they walked over together. He bent down to grab it quickly, but the shirt wouldn't budge. Tegan tugged in frustration. "How is this still stuck?"

Yanay crouched down. "It's not hooked. The whole back is glued to these roots. It's like they're covered with some kind of sap."

The others rose and crowded close. The twisting mass of exposed roots gleamed in the glow of their flashlights, as if they were wet. Tegan picked up a small branch and touched it to one of the roots. It stuck fast.

Marcus turned to Yanay. "What kind of tree has sappy roots?"

Her clouded expression looked eerie in the flickering firelight. "I don't know. Sap is usually on the trunk and only in small amounts. But these roots are coated with it. They're sticky everywhere, almost like . . ." She trailed off, looking uncomfortable.

Ning spoke in a grim voice. "Almost like spiderwebs?"

CHAPTER 15

THE CREATURE retreated into the comforting darkness, far from the dreaded flames.

Tense with frustration, it tried to relax its body. Its prey had been so close. If only the tall one hadn't thrust with the fire stick. It hadn't expected that.

The creature rubbed its jaw, creating an eerie chirping sound.

Next time, it would be ready.

CHAPTER 16

TEGAN LAY awake for hours that night, wishing he had his cat, Buford, to cuddle with. He kept slapping at imaginary spiders crawling over his skin. When he did sleep, huge eyes haunted his dreams.

At daybreak, he crawled wearily from his tent to find the others already stirring. He zipped on his sweatshirt, which he'd finally freed last night with help from Marcus and Ning. The sky was streaked with pink and orange, and the nutty smell of coffee wafted from a pot over the campfire. Tegan had to pee but wasn't brave enough to wander into the half-light beneath the trees.

Ed walked over to where they'd seen the eyes. "No tracks. The ground's too rocky."

Yanay joined him and examined the twisted grid of roots. "This sap is so strange."

"Now we have weird stones *and* mysteriously sticky roots," Ed said. "Our 'unexplained' list is growing."

"Don't forget the missing trail markers," Marcus said.

"And giant eyeballs," Ning added.

Tegan's troubled thoughts drifted to his mom, wishing for the hundredth time that she was here. He could use a hug. Was she worried about him? She certainly would be if she knew the mess they were in.

Yanay stood up, looking uneasy. She checked her map and compass again before throwing them in her pack with a frustrated sigh. "Let's get moving."

They left camp and hiked south. As sore as Tegan felt, Yanay's prediction was coming true—he was getting stronger, and their packs were growing lighter. But that also meant their food supply was dwindling.

They were hiking along a towering cliff when Marcus spied a wide ledge high on the rock face. "Wish we could get up there. We might be able to see the trail."

"Last I checked, Spider-Man wasn't with us," Ed said.

Ning shrugged. "I am."

Moving to the base of the cliff, she looked up and pantomimed moves with her hands, mapping out a route in her head. Satisfied, she took off her pack and pulled out her climbing shoes.

"Whoa," Yanay said. "Not a good idea."

Ning sat down and began unlacing her hiking boots. "Mom. It's barely thirty feet, and there's a good route. At most, it's a five-point-nine. I've done way harder climbs than that."

"In a gym with someone belaying you," Yanay said. "Not free soloing."

"See how the ground slopes away from the cliff?" Ning asked. "Marcus is right—I might be able to see the trail from up there."

Yanay bit her lip. "I don't like it. What if you fall?"

Ning stood and placed her hands on Yanay's shoulders. "If I get to a spot I'm not comfortable with, I'll come down. Promise." She paused. "We're lost. Let me help."

Finally, Yanay gave a reluctant nod.

Ning hugged her, and Ed glanced down, as if the display of affection made him uncomfortable. She pulled a chalk bag from her pack and clicked the nylon strap around her waist. Ning did some light stretches and approached the wall. After chalking both hands, she jumped up and caught a small ledge. Her feet found bumps in the rock, and she clung to the cliff like a spider. She flexed her knees and, with a quick burst, launched herself up and caught a higher ledge. Yanay blew out a nervous breath.

Dangling from her new grip, Ning slipped one foot into a vertical crevice. She placed her other foot on a nub of rock and pulled herself onto the ledge she'd been hanging from. After shaking out her hands, she quickly scaled a bumpy section of wall to a large V-shaped crevice. Wedging herself inside, she worked her way up to the underside of the lookout ledge.

"That ledge sticks out from the wall," Marcus whispered to Tegan. "How's she gonna get past the overhang?"

Tegan shook his head, feeling as nervous as Yanay looked. He'd seen Ning make amazing moves in climbing competitions, but this was different.

Ning paused for a moment, examining the underside of the ledge. She reached out and gripped one handhold, then slowly found a second. With her feet still in the crevice, she now hung almost parallel to the ground nearly thirty feet up. Yanay stared at her shoes, but Tegan's eyes were frozen on Ning, his heart lodged in his throat.

As Ning reached up and grabbed the top of the ledge, the projection under her right foot broke away, leaving her leg dangling in midair. The unexpected shift in balance caused her left foot to slip, leaving her suspended by her fingertips beneath the ledge.

Stunningly, Ning didn't panic. She gathered herself and swung her foot up to a small shelf of rock.

After a few more anxious moments, she hauled herself onto the ledge.

The watching group gave an audible sigh of relief. Yanay walked a few steps away and shook herself like a cat emerging from water. Ning's head appeared, her face flushed with exertion. She waved down before disappearing from view.

A few minutes later, Ning carefully made her way down the cliff. As soon as her feet hit the ground, Yanay pulled her into a bear hug.

"I'm fine, Mom," Ning said, rolling her eyes.

"Great climb," Tegan said. "Did you see the trail?"

She shook her head grimly. "No. But I found something strange, though. In the center of the ledge was a pile of those weird rocks."

CHAPTER 17

FOR THE rest of the morning, they maneuvered hills, cliffs, and streams with no sign of the elusive trail. Tegan passed the time by examining trees, looking for the right sapling for a bow and straight branches for arrows. He'd learned how make them at archery camp the previous summer, and ever since the incident with the mysterious eyes, having some kind of weapon sounded comforting. When he found the needed supplies, Yanay cut them down with her survival knife.

They were a dispirited group as they broke for lunch, munching on trail mix and jerky. Ed moved off to go to the bathroom while Yanay scouted ahead.

Marcus watched her slip through the trees. "Your mom's awesome."

"You don't have to live with her," Ning said.

Tegan looked over in surprise. "I thought you two were close."

"We are. She's my best friend and everything—"

Marcus feigned being stabbed in the chest. "Ouch. Would you like your knife back?"

Ning pushed him playfully. "Besides you two dorks. It's just that she gets really protective, and it bugs me sometimes."

"At least she cares," Tegan said. "Unlike my dad."

Marcus nodded. "And I bet she'll support whatever you pick for a career. Unlike my parents."

Ning tilted her head to one side. "I guess you're right. She is pretty great."

After confirming he still had no cell service, Tegan lay back and daydreamed about a Godzilla burger and a salted caramel milkshake from the Sugarbowl, his favorite ice cream place. He planned to work there when he turned sixteen—free ice cream sounded like the ultimate job perk, and he'd use the money to buy his aunt Jackie's 1974 Mustang.

As Ed and Yanay returned, Tegan spotted an unusual pattern on a massive oak across the clearing. Wandering over, he found matching pairs of holes in the thick bark, each about two inches in diameter. They ran side by side up the trunk before disappearing into the branches high above.

"What's with these holes?" he asked.

Marcus stepped forward eagerly to examine them. "Woodpeckers and insects can make holes in tree bark, but I've never seen them in pairs like this. How about you, Mrs. Chen?"

Yanay peered closely at the holes, tracing one

with her fingers. "It almost seems like they were punched into the wood by something sharp. Maybe a logger's climbing spikes?"

"This is a national forest," Ed said. "There hasn't been logging here for decades."

Ning studied the towering tree. "I'm gonna see where they lead." She slipped on her climbing shoes and chalk bag.

"How can you climb this?" Marcus asked. "The first limbs are way too high."

Ning tugged experimentally on the rough bark. "Laybacking should work."

She hooked the fingers of both hands at waist height in a vertical seam of thick bark. Leaning back, she placed one foot, then the other against the trunk. She was now bent over and clinging to the side of the tree, her body perpendicular to the trunk.

"*Please* be careful," Yanay said, hugging herself.

By shifting her fingers higher up the seam in the

bark and placing one foot above the other, Ning moved smoothly up the tree. Tegan shook his head. When it came to climbing, Ning was pretty amazing.

She pulled herself onto the lowest limb and shifted from branch to branch until she disappeared from view.

A minute ticked by.

"You okay?" Yanay shouted.

Moments later, Ning appeared and gave the okay sign before climbing down. She landed beside them like a cat, breathing hard.

"Learn anything?" Marcus asked.

"Yeah," Ning said. "The holes stop above those thick branches. And I found this caught on a limb." She pulled something from her pocket and held it out.

It was an orange trail tag.

CHAPTER 18

THEY STARED in disbelief at the tag in Ning's hand.

"But . . . how?" Tegan sputtered. "And why?"

"Good questions," Yanay said as she gazed up the tree, her brow wrinkled. "These holes are fresh. Who could have made them?"

"Who or *what*?" Marcus asked.

"Are you thinking about those eyes from last night?" Tegan asked.

Marcus nodded. "I just remembered something.

There's a creature with two hooked claws on each foot that help it climb. Any guesses?"

Tegan felt like he'd swallowed twenty ice cubes. "Please say 'sloth.'"

"Are you saying these holes were made by the claws of a *spider*?" Ed asked.

"Not necessarily," Marcus replied. "Like I said before, I'm only trying to come up with a theory that fits the facts. One, we saw eight big eyes that moved like they belonged to a single creature. Two, Tegan's shirt was stuck to a weblike coating on some roots. Three, these holes weren't made by anything else we can think of. One possible explanation for those facts, however wild it sounds, is that this forest is home to a monster spider." He looked at each of them. "I'm open to other ideas. I *really* want to be wrong here."

"Um . . . how about 'monster spiders don't

exist'?" Ning said. "I mean, what's the biggest known spider?"

"By weight, the Goliath birdeater tarantula," said Marcus. "By leg span, the giant huntsman. It's about the size of a dinner plate."

Tegan shuddered. "First of all, eww. Secondly, that's huge, but it's nothing compared to what we're talking about here."

"True," said Marcus. "This would be something completely unknown. Like the *T. rex* of spiders."

Tegan stared warily at the surrounding forest. "If it's okay with everybody, I'd like to go home now."

"No argument from me," Ning said.

"Marcus, you think like a scientist, which is wonderful," Yanay said, "but finding a theory that fits the facts doesn't make it true."

"Do you have another idea?" Ning asked.

Yanay looked uncomfortable. "Not yet."

"Okay, so for now, we're going with 'we're all gonna die'?" Tegan asked.

"No one's gonna die," Ed said, then shrugged. "Probably."

"Ed!" Yanay glared at him.

"I'm kidding, I'm kidding." He held up his hands apologetically. "I'm sure there's a rational explanation that doesn't involve monsters."

CHAPTER 19

THAT NIGHT, they set up camp in a large clearing and clustered their tents as far from the trees as possible. Ning made a big campfire, and as darkness fell, they huddled close to the comforting flames. Tegan was relieved that his normally clueless dad didn't attempt a scary story—reality was scary enough.

Their forced efforts at conversation died out quickly, and they sat awkwardly avoiding eye contact. Marcus was absorbed in examining another of the mysterious stones he'd found and brought into camp. Tegan worked steadily on the section of sapling he'd cut for a bow, stripping the bark from one side and narrowing the ends with Yanay's knife, leaving the middle thicker for strength. Time crawled, but no one seemed in a hurry to separate into their tents.

Finally, Yanay stood. "We need sleep for another long hike tomorrow. Hopefully, we'll find the trail and get out of here."

Reluctantly, Tegan grabbed the camp shovel and was about to throw dirt on the fire when Ning grabbed his arm, causing the dirt to land on his boot.

"What the—" he began irritably, but stopped when he noticed the look on Ning's face.

"Shhh," she whispered. "Listen."

They all froze, ears straining.

"I don't hear anything," Tegan said.

"That's the problem."

Then it hit him. The normal forest noises were missing. No scampering of small animals, no cracking of twigs, no calls of night birds. Only the breeze whispering in the trees.

With an icy hiss, a huge shape pushed its way into the firelight.

Tegan's mind went blank, unable to process what he was seeing. It was a spider, yet it couldn't be a spider. A spider shouldn't be the size of a horse. Double rows of huge eyes gleamed in the firelight. Eight multijointed legs, each bristling with stiff brown hair, arched high above its swollen abdomen. Each foot was tipped with a pair of wickedly curved claws. Flexible appendages on either side of the creature's massive fangs swayed slowly as if testing the air.

For a heart-stopping moment, no one moved.

Then Tegan screamed, long and loud and piercing. All the terror inside him found its horrible voice.

The spider surged forward and raised a clawed leg toward Marcus as he stumbled back with a screech, his eyes locked on the monster. For its huge size, the spider was incredibly fast, but Ning was faster. Snatching up her thick walking stick, she slammed it into the monster's outstretched claw. With a hiss of rage, the spider flicked one long leg into Ning's shoulder, sending her tumbling away.

Every nerve in Tegan's body screamed at him to run, but his feet wouldn't respond. Ed sat frozen on the ground, his face a horrified mask. With a primal yell, Yanay grabbed a rock from the firepit and launched it at the spider's head. An unearthly shriek of pain and anger tore through the night as one massive eye crumpled and went dark. The monster hefted its body off the ground, front legs clawing the air like a demented stallion.

A moment later, it crashed back to earth. Marcus tried to scramble away, but the spider thrust its nightmarish head over him, reaching out with jointed appendages. His shrill cry of terror broke Tegan's paralysis. Tegan grabbed a burning stick from the fire and jabbed it at the monster's face.

The spider scuttled backward, its cluster of eyes locked on the flaming branch. Tegan jabbed again as Marcus hurriedly crawled behind him. Ning and Yanay snatched up burning sticks and closed in on the spider. It hesitated. Then with a flash of motion, it darted forward and scrabbled at the ground.

With a final hiss, the monster turned and vanished into the night.

CHAPTER 20

FOR SEVERAL long moments, the only sounds were ragged breathing and the crackling of the fire.

The five looked at one another in horrified disbelief, their faces streaked with sweat. Tegan slumped to the ground, his legs like sand. Tears he didn't remember crying ran down his cheeks. Everyone instinctively huddled close to the fire, staring into the darkness that had swallowed the spider.

"Is everybody okay?" Yanay asked in a shaky voice. She put a hand on Ning's shoulder and winced.

"You're not," Ning said. "Let me see your hand."

Yanay's palm was red and blistered from the firepit rock. Ning took a first aid kit from Yanay's backpack and cleaned her mom's hand. She applied burn cream and wrapped it in a cloth bandage.

"Looks like you were right, Marcus," Yanay said.

He nodded slowly, his eyes still locked on the space where the monster had disappeared. "Sorry about that."

"Anybody else need patching up?" Ning asked. "How about you, Mr. Campbell? Mr. Campbell?"

Ed sat nearby, a slack expression on his face. He hadn't spoken since the spider had appeared. Tegan stared at him, remembering what his father did during the attack—nothing. Nothing at all. Tegan turned away as a familiar feeling of embarrassment welled up in his gut. If his mom was here, she'd have been the first to try to protect them. Given his dad's fear of spiders, seeing that monster must have been truly terrifying. But it was terrifying for all of them. Tegan set his jaw. *He* was facing his fears out here—his dad could grow up and do the same.

Ed stirred as if coming out of a trance. "What? Uh . . . yeah, I'm okay. Sure."

Yanay gave him a frustrated glance. "Thanks for the help," she muttered before addressing the group. "Now that we know what we're dealing with, our first priority is keeping ourselves safe."

"But how do we do that?" Tegan asked, his voice cracking in fear. "That thing can walk into camp anytime it wants!"

An uncomfortable silence fell.

"Understanding the spider is our best defense," Marcus said. "What do we know?"

"It's huge and wants to kill us," Ning said.

"Besides that," Marcus said. "We've only seen it at night, right? If it's nocturnal, that means we're probably safe during the day."

"A lot of big predators are," Yanay said. "We also know its eyes are vulnerable."

"Fire," Ning said. "The eyes disappeared last night when I approached with a flaming stick, and it backed off when Tegan jabbed at it."

"And left when you two joined me with more fire," Tegan said.

"Now we're getting somewhere," Marcus said, his excitement growing. "It's active at night, its eyes are weak spots, and it doesn't like fire."

"Why did it take the stone?" Ed asked quietly.

They turned toward him as he gazed blankly into the flames. His face was sickly pale.

"I . . . I didn't know it had," Marcus said. He searched the area where he'd been examining the mysterious rock when the spider had attacked.

The stone was gone.

CHAPTER 21

FEAR OF the spider returning hovered over them like a poisonous fog. They banked the campfire and took turns keeping watch. Not wanting to be alone in their tents, they laid their sleeping bags around the protective flames.

The forest sounds returned, and the rest of the night passed quietly. In the morning, they packed quickly, eager to continue their search for the trail. No one wanted to face another night in that menacing forest.

Conversation was limited as they hiked. They were exhausted and kept glancing nervously in every direction. The monster seemed to be nocturnal, but no one was willing to bet their life on it.

"I've been thinking about those holes in the tree," Marcus said as they shared a meager lunch of dried fruit and nuts. "Since they match the spider's claws, we can assume the spider made them, right?"

"Sounds reasonable," Yanay said.

"Ning found one of the missing orange trail tags in the same tree," Marcus continued. "So if the spider made the holes . . ."

Yanay glanced up sharply. "You think the *spider* took the trail tags?"

Tegan's eyes widened. "But if it purposely removed those markers, that would mean—"

"It knew what they were," Ning said, a tremor in her voice. "It took them to trap us."

"That means the spider's intelligent," Marcus

said, pushing his glasses higher on his nose. "*Very* intelligent."

Tegan put his head in his hands. "Like it wasn't terrifying enough already."

They struggled on, constantly adjusting their route to head south. As the afternoon wore away, Yanay led them up a barren slope.

"Shouldn't we be down in the forest looking for a flat spot to camp?" Ning asked.

Yanay scanned the surrounding cliffs. "I was hoping to find a cave."

"A cave would be much easier to defend," Marcus said.

Yanay checked the sun, which was already dipping close to the mountain ridge. "Help me look. I don't want to be out in the open after nightfall."

Over the next hour, they climbed to various spots that looked promising from a distance, only to find them too small or choked with brambles and debris.

Yanay sighed. "If we don't find something in the next ten minutes, we'll have to camp in the trees."

"What about there?" Ed asked, pointing down the rocky slope they were crossing. Tegan glanced at him in surprise. His dad had been almost silent the entire day. Normally, Tegan would have been thrilled with the change in Ed—the less he talked, the less likely he was to embarrass himself or Tegan. But now it felt unsettling.

Below a short drop-off was the edge of a dark opening. Ning jogged over and peered down. "It looks good!"

They scrambled to the level of the cave. The opening was about fifteen feet wide, and just deep enough to fit them all.

"Good find, Ed," Yanay said. "Now we need to

hustle. Why don't you and Tegan gather firewood while the rest of us set up camp? And be careful."

He nodded. "Come on, T."

Ed and Tegan dropped their packs beside the cave and headed into the brush. Twilight was deepening. Moving quickly, they gathered as much wood as they could carry. On the way back, Tegan spied another oval rock between the roots of a giant oak.

After dropping the wood at the edge of the cave, Tegan rolled out his sleeping bag. He kept thinking about the stone he'd just seen, remembering its mottled gray surface and the odd feel of the one he'd touched. Why had the spider taken the stone from their camp?

Tegan sucked in a sharp breath as his eyes went wide. He grabbed the small camp shovel and turned to Marcus. "Be right back." Before he could talk himself out of it, Tegan darted into the nearby trees.

"Wait!" Marcus called.

Tegan ignored him and retraced his steps. After a few minutes of nervous searching, he finally spotted the stone beneath the tree. Dropping to his knees, he quickly dug away the dirt, and with a tug, it came loose in his hands. Tucking the shovel under his arm, Tegan hefted the stone and hurried back.

Everyone was outside the cave looking for him when he returned.

"Tegan, no one should go off by themselves," Yanay said with a deep frown. "It's not safe."

"I know, I'm sorry," he said. "But I think it's important."

"What's important?" Ning asked.

"This." Tegan raised the stone over his head and slammed it down on the rocky ground.

The stone split open with a dull crunch, releasing a thick greenish-yellow goo.

"What the . . . ?" Ed said.

In the middle of the mess lay the curled body of a large spider.

CHAPTER 22

"THEY'RE *EGGS*," Ning said with a shudder of disgust. "Monster spider eggs."

"Of course!" Marcus said. "Why didn't I see it before?"

"Don't beat yourself up," Yanay said. "They look so much like rocks. Nice work, Tegan."

"That explains why the spider took the one we had last night," Ed said. "It was protecting its egg."

"Maybe that's why it attacked us in the first place," Ning said.

Hope swelled in Tegan. "So we should be safe tonight since we don't have one of its eggs!"

"Except the one you just destroyed," Marcus said. As a huge animal lover, he felt almost sorry for the creature. Then he remembered it would have grown into a ruthless killer.

The balloon in Tegan's chest popped. "Oops."

"We'll build a big fire at the entrance," Yanay said as she grabbed five long sticks from the back of the cave. "And I scrounged these earlier."

"Too big for roasting marshmallows," Ning said.

"But not too big for spears," Yanay replied.

"Yes!" Marcus said. "We can use them to hold off the spider if it gets past the fire."

Yanay pulled out her survival knife. She took a stick and demonstrated how to sharpen one end with steady, controlled strokes. "Be careful. Like I told Tegan, it's really sharp. Once we get the fire going, we can harden the tips in the flames."

While Ning built up the fire, the others took turns sharpening their spears. Marcus seemed excited, a feeling Tegan didn't share. Given the relatively short length of the spears, they'd have to be close to the monster to use them. An image of its unblinking eyes, enormous fangs, and wicked-looking claws came to Tegan's mind with brutal clarity. He shuddered, not wanting to be anywhere near that nightmare again.

Tegan helped his dad rummage through their rapidly diminishing food supply. They ate mac and cheese along with the last of the thick chocolate, now melted into a glob. Tegan held his portion on his tongue, savoring the sweetness and wondering when he'd taste it again.

With the moon shrouded by clouds, the forest beyond their campfire was completely black. The flickering firelight threw dancing shadows on the stone walls. The group had settled into a comfortable silence, feeling much safer in the cave than they did in the open.

Tegan worked at his bow, carving notches for the bowstring at each end and whittling the points on his arrows. Turning to Marcus, he asked, "Have you collected any bird feathers for your science project?"

Marcus narrowed his eyes suspiciously. "Yeah, some really cool ones. Why?"

Tegan held up his arrows. "They won't fly straight without fletching."

"What's fletching?" Ning asked.

"The feathers on the backs of arrows," Tegan said. He turned to Marcus. "I know your science project is really important to you, but having weapons is pretty important right now too. Think I could use those feathers?"

Marcus frowned, obviously not wanting to sacrifice any of his project, but unable to argue with

Tegan's logic. He pulled out two large feathers with a sigh and handed them over.

Tegan cut the long feathers into sections and split them along their quills. Using twine from Yanay's pack, he tied three pieces to the end of each arrow.

Suddenly Ning gasped and snatched up her spear. In the darkness beyond the cave entrance, seven huge eyes gleamed in the firelight. For all its bulk, the monster had approached with incredible stealth. It stood motionless to the left of the flames, its features hidden. The eye damaged by Yanay's rock was lost in shadow. They all scrambled up and held out their spears.

The combatants stared at each other, with only the crackling fire breaking the silence.

To the right of the flames, a *second* set of gleaming orbs appeared. Eight more enormous eyes.

Marcus groaned, and the spear shook in his

hands. Tegan broke out in a cold sweat as half-digested mac and cheese roiled nauseatingly in his gut.

The monsters attacked.

Twin hideous faces filled the entrance to the cave, the firelight framing them in a garish glow. Stiff brown hair bristled around their huge fangs and covered their swollen bodies. On either side of their jaws, matching feelers swayed hypnotically like cobras ready to strike.

Ning surged forward and thrust her spear at the second spider's head. An angry hiss filled the air as it scuttled backward. The first spider shot its leg into the cave and caught Marcus behind his knees. He fell back, his spear clattering to the stone floor. Tegan rushed to help, but the spider hooked its claw on Marcus's jeans and yanked him away.

Marcus screamed in terror as he slid along the ground toward the monster. He kicked wildly, trying to free himself. One foot slammed into the fire, scattering burning logs across the ground.

As Marcus reached the cave opening, Tegan pulled the sleeve of his sweatshirt over his hand like a makeshift glove. Reaching down, he picked up a flaming log and hurled it into the spider's face.

The impact sent sparks shooting into the night. The monster roared, its jaws spread wide, revealing more of its enormous fangs. It released Marcus and swiped at the smoldering embers on its head. Tegan helped Marcus back into the cave, while Ning and Yanay took turns darting forward, using their spears to keep the second spider at bay. Ed remained at the rear of the cave, his spear held out weakly in front of him, eyes glazed with terror.

The second spider turned toward the first with a loud chittering sound. A moment later, all the eyes winked out. The monsters were gone.

CHAPTER 23

TEGAN TRIED to flee, but his path was blocked by rows of giant eyes. He scrambled desperately in the opposite direction, only to encounter more eyes, these dripping blood. His breath came in ragged gasps as his heart smashed against his ribs. The spiders advanced slowly, then leaped toward him, massive fangs raised and appendages waving. One of them grabbed Tegan's shoulder with a piercing claw and began to shake him. Drowning in waves of terror, he threw back his head and screamed—

"Tegan!" Ning said as she shook his shoulder. "Wake up."

He sat up like a shot, looking around wildly. "Wha . . . ? Ning?"

"It's okay," she said. "You were having a bad dream. Come on, we're packing up."

Pale morning light filled the cave. The others were moving around the remains of last night's fire, stowing gear. Tegan lowered his forehead to his knees—even sleep was no escape from this living nightmare.

He stood slowly as his aching muscles groaned in protest, and vowed to never take his bed for granted again. If he ever got the chance.

Yanay handed him a protein bar. "We're going to eat as we go to get a jump on the trail search. You doing okay?"

Tegan began to nod automatically, then stopped. "Not really."

Yanay gave him a sad smile. "I guess none of us are, huh? If you want to talk about it, I'm here."

"Thanks." Tegan glanced at his dad. Why wasn't *he* saying things like that? But who was Tegan kidding? Ed just didn't care about him. He could handle this situation so much better if his mom was here.

When the gear was packed and the fire doused, they gathered at the front of the cave. Yanay faced them with a somber expression. "There's no denying that our bad situation just got a whole lot worse."

"How could there be *two* of them?" Ning asked.

"It makes sense," Marcus said. "Given the eggs, there must be a mating pair."

Tegan's face crinkled. "Eww."

"Yeah, well, I wish the female had killed the male once she was pregnant," Ning said bitterly.

"You're thinking of black widows," Marcus said.

"These looked more like dino-sized huntsman spiders. Huntsmans are skilled predators." He hesitated a moment, looking uncomfortable. "Sorry to say it, but I think we're lucky something worse didn't happen last night."

Tegan blew out a breath. "That really cheered me up."

"The cave certainly helped," Yanay said. "I hate leaving it."

"But if we don't keep going, we'll never find the trail," Ning said.

Yanay nodded. "Our food is running low too, and even with the portable phone chargers, there's still no cell service. If we don't make it back on schedule, the rangers will search for us. But that could take time, and with the trail markers gone, we'll be tough to find."

"We could try a signal fire on a ridge," Ning suggested. "A spotter plane might see it."

"Good thought, but there won't be a search plane for days yet, and a fire big enough to catch someone's attention before then would be too risky. In these dry conditions, we could trap ourselves in a forest fire." Yanay gave a grim smile. "Sorry to be so gloomy."

"It's okay," Marcus said. "I'd rather know the truth."

"Yeah, thanks for being honest with us," Ning said.

"You deserve that much," Yanay said. "You've all proven you can handle a really tough situation, better than some adults."

Ed shifted uncomfortably and stared off into the trees.

"We'd better get moving," Yanay said finally.

As Tegan shouldered his pack, something caught his eye. Or the lack of something. "Hey, where's the egg?"

Everyone looked where he'd smashed the egg the night before. It was gone.

"Scavengers?" Marcus said. "That unborn spider goo would be a tempting snack."

"But the shell pieces are gone too," Ning said. "Scavengers wouldn't eat the shell."

After a puzzled silence, Ed spoke. "Looks like when Mom and Dad left last night, they took their little monster."

CHAPTER 24

"WELL, IT'S . . . interesting," Ning said during an afternoon break as Tegan admired his completed bow and arrows. He'd just finished stringing the bow with twine.

"Does it work?" asked Marcus.

"Of course," Tegan said, a little too defensively. "I mean, I think so."

"Go on," Ning said. "Take a shot."

Tegan spied a fallen tree that made a good target. Moving closer, he nocked an arrow on the string, careful not to disturb the feathers. Standing with his left shoulder toward his target, Tegan raised the bow and drew back the string until his thumb touched his cheek. A drop of nervous sweat dripped into his eye as he felt the stares of his audience. Taking a deep breath, he steadied his aim and released the arrow.

It limped weakly through the air and fell to the ground well short of the target.

Ed laughed. "Those spiders better watch out! We've got Legolas here."

Tegan's face fell faster than the arrow. Wordlessly, he marched across the clearing and threw down his bow before dropping onto a log. A few moments later, Ning sat beside him.

"Ignore him," she said. "That was a great first try."

"Easy for you to say. Your mom actually likes you."

"Your dad likes you too. He's just not great at showing it."

"He's not great at showing much," Tegan said. "Except what a coward he is. Did you see him during the spider attacks? I'm surprised he didn't wet himself."

"I'm surprised *I* didn't wet myself," Ning said. "You're right, Ed didn't do a lot, but not everybody reacts the same way in tough situations."

"But at least the rest of us tried! Even me, and I'm the weakest one here."

"You're small, but that doesn't make you weak. And don't give up on your dad. He might surprise you."

Tegan laughed bitterly. "I doubt it."

"Come on. You should keep practicing." She handed him the bow with a sly smile. "Megan Franklin will never have a crush on a quitter."

Blushing furiously, Tegan started to protest. Then he sighed and positioned himself in front of the target again. He shot his dad a dark look, but Ed seemed oblivious. *Nothing new there,* Tegan thought. Ed's cluelessness about feelings was really sad, and for a moment, Tegan almost felt sorry for him.

The moment passed. *Grow up, Dad.*

CHAPTER 25

"STORM'S COMING," Ed said late that afternoon, his face craned skyward.

Dark clouds swept by like gray ghosts. Below, everything was still, but overhead, the treetops creaked and swayed in a slow dance.

Yanay pinched the bridge of her nose and blew out a sharp breath. "Why can't I find that blasted trail?!"

Marcus glanced at Tegan, his eyebrows raised.

Seeing a crack in Yanay's calm positivity unnerved them both.

Ning drew her mom into a hug. "It's okay."

Yanay let herself be held before she pulled back and gazed at Ning, her eyes moist. "I'm the one who's supposed to be comforting you."

"You've done plenty of that," Ning said. "I can take a turn."

Ed watched their exchange with a sorrowful expression. He glanced at Tegan, then looked away and cleared his throat. "The light's fading. We'd better find a place to camp and get a fire going."

Squaring her shoulders, Yanay led them forward. Soon she stopped in a small clearing choked with fallen trees. "Not as good as a cave, but this downed wood might give us some protection."

They broke into their now routine jobs of collecting wood, preparing a firepit, and setting up tents.

"At least we don't have to go far this time," Marcus said as he and Tegan gathered sticks from the surrounding debris.

Tegan glanced uneasily at the deep shadows in the surrounding forest. "Definitely better than searching in there."

A few minutes later, they staggered back to the campsite. As Tegan dumped the wood beside the ring of stones Ning had arranged, he noticed one of the fallen trees nearby. The exposed roots spiraled out from the upturned base higher than Tegan's head, creating an eerie pattern in the gathering gloom.

Soon the tents were arranged, and Ning had the fire crackling brightly. In the distance, a fork of lightning split the sky between two mountain peaks. Five seconds later came a deep boom of thunder.

"The storm's about a mile away," Marcus said.

"How do you know that?" Tegan asked.

"Count the seconds between the lightning and

thunder, then divide by five," Marcus said. "The shorter the gap, the closer the storm."

The dull glow of the shrouded sun dipped behind the mountains. With the moon and stars hidden, darkness fell like a hammer. As Tegan huddled closer to the fire, he spied subtle movement on the far side of the clearing. At the edge of the firelight was the oddly shaped cluster of exposed roots he'd noticed earlier.

As Tegan watched, one of the roots began to move. It swayed slightly and bent as if jointed. The blood rushed from Tegan's head, and his stomach flopped like a beached fish. *It's the wind,* he thought desperately. *It has to be.* Then a second root stretched in the opposite direction. So much for the wind.

Lightning flashed again. Three seconds later came the clap of thunder. The storm was getting closer. Tegan's mouth went desert dry, turning his words into a gasp.

"You okay?" Ning asked.

He pointed a quivering finger.

Ning followed his gaze, and her eyes swelled like balloons. "Mo-o-o-m . . ."

The rest of the group turned to look. Some of the long roots were bending freely in multiple places. A tremor ran through the roundish clump near the ground. Above it, a smaller section lifted and swung stiffly like a gate on rusted hinges. Attached to it were two large, triangular points with a branch waving sluggishly on either side.

With a slow twisting motion, the entire mass detached itself from the base of the tree.

Tegan sat frozen in place, unable to move, to look away, to breathe.

The giant spider glared at them with eight massive eyes.

CHAPTER 26

TEGAN STARED at the monster in disbelief as the wind howled through the trees. A brilliant flash of lightning chased away the darkness, quickly followed by chest-rattling thunder.

Tegan's brain felt stuck. Impossible as it seemed, the creepy mass of tree roots had been disguising one of the monster spiders. The urge to flee was almost overwhelming, but he knew this was a nightmare he couldn't outrun.

Marcus leaped up and held out his spear. Ning

and Yanay snatched burning sticks from the fire and waved them at the monster, their shouts lost in the swirling wind. After reaching for his spear, Tegan hesitated and picked up his bow instead. He tried to nock an arrow, but his hands were shaking too badly.

Clutching his spear, Ed struggled to his feet and turned to face the spider. Seeing the movement, it fixed him with a deadly gaze. Ed's knees buckled, and he sat heavily.

The spider moved slowly from side to side but made no attempt to come forward. *What's it waiting for?* Tegan thought. *Is it that afraid of the fire?*

The realization hit him an instant too late.

He spun around to find the second spider nearly on top of him. The first had kept the group's attention, allowing its mate to approach from their blind side. Tegan stumbled back with a scream, firing wildly as he fell. The arrow flew wide, and the spider loomed over him, fangs poised.

Ning turned and hurled her flaming stick at the monster's head. The spider shrieked and fell back as a shower of sparks rained down, singeing Tegan's face. Grabbing her spear, Ning ran over as Tegan scrambled to his feet. He dropped his bow and picked up Ning's fallen firebrand. Together they jabbed at the second spider, while behind them, Marcus and Yanay did the same with the first.

"Ed!" Yanay shouted fiercely. "We need you!"

Tegan saw his dad pick up his spear and get unsteadily to his feet. Ed tried to force himself into the action, only to sway where he stood, feebly pointing his weapon first at one spider, then the other.

A duo of lightning and thunder exploded directly above them, triggering a sudden burst of cold rain. The wind raged, and Tegan struggled to keep his footing on the suddenly slick ground. The darkness seemed to be deepening somehow, making it harder to dodge the swipes of the spider's long, clawed legs. *How is it getting darker?* he thought numbly.

And then, yielding to the relentless storm, the fire went out.

CHAPTER 27

TWIN SHRIEKS cut through the howling wind as the spiders celebrated the dousing of the fire.

The flaming sticks Yanay and Tegan held faded to a dull glow. A flashlight came to life, revealing Yanay, her long dark hair plastered to her face by the rain. Ning grabbed her light and flicked it on.

The spiders attacked.

"Run!" Yanay screamed.

Tegan tried to obey but tripped, his feet tangled in his bow. His face slammed into the ground, stunning him. As Ning hauled him to his feet, he grabbed his bow and arrows. They fled across the clearing, following the bobbing of Yanay's flashlight. Ed and Marcus, whose pack dangled from his shoulder, scrambled along beside them. The group ducked in and out of the jumble of logs, trying to dodge the pursuing spiders.

A hairy leg crashed down in front of Tegan, its sharp claws sinking deep into the wet earth. He and Ning dove sideways and crawled through a gap between logs. As she started to rise, he yanked her down. Huge fangs swept the air above her.

"Get to the trees!" Yanay cried.

Moments later, they all darted into a tight cluster of pines. The spiders slammed furiously against the thick trunks, unable to fit into the confined space. Everyone jumped back as the monsters reached in with their legs, claws probing.

"We need a cave!" Marcus yelled.

"Follow me!" Yanay called.

They burst from the far side of the cluster, fighting to stay together in the black forest. They ran wildly, ducking branches and pushing through tangled brush. Skirting the ring of trees, the spiders crashed after them, gaining ground.

Yanay found a game trail, and the group surged forward in a ragged line. Ahead, two slender trees bent toward each other, forming an archway over the trail. Beyond loomed a rocky cliff.

"Through here!" Yanay yelled back as she reached the tree arch. "I think I see—"

A hideous head appeared at the top of the archway. Seven eyes gleamed wickedly in the glow of Yanay's flashlight. Quick as lightning, a jointed leg swung down and snatched Yanay off her feet.

Tegan gave a choked cry of horror. The arch wasn't formed by trees—it was the gap between the back legs of a third monster spider. It had been standing upright, holding its body off the ground by clinging to the trees while straddling the trail and waiting for them to run beneath it.

Holding Yanay aloft in its front legs, the spider dropped heavily to the ground, then turned and scuttled into the darkness at frightening speed. A long, heart-wrenching scream faded into the distance.

"Nooo!" Ning cried in anguish. "Mom!"

Yanay was gone.

CHAPTER 28

FOR A moment, they all stood paralyzed with shock. Then Ning snatched up Yanay's fallen flashlight and thrust it at Marcus. "Come on!"

Marcus and Tegan moved to follow her but were yanked back. Tegan whirled in surprise to see Ed with a firm grip on their shirts.

"What are you doing?" Tegan yelled. "We have to help Yanay!"

"Look at the cliff!" Ed shouted.

Tegan turned. A flashlight beam revealed the dark opening of a cave. "But Yanay!"

"No time!" Ed glanced over his shoulder.

Multiple stabs of lightning lit the forest like a strobe. The two spiders raced up the trail behind them. Ed pushed Tegan and Marcus toward the cave opening. Grabbing Ning's arm, he dragged her along as she struggled to run after Yanay.

They scrambled up a rocky slope and crammed themselves into the low cave. Pressed against the back wall, they shined their lights at the entrance. The spiders crowded the too-small opening, screeching in fury. A long leg shot into the space, sweeping wildly. Marcus cracked it above the claws with his spear, and the leg retreated.

"My mom!" Ning sobbed. "We have to help my mom!"

"We can't do anything right now," Ed said. "Not with those things out there."

Tegan took her hand. "Ning, listen to me. We're *going* to go after her. We will, but . . . not now. I hate it, but my dad's right."

"At sunrise those things should be gone," Marcus said. "Then we can search. We'll find her, I promise."

Ning glared at them, her eyes wild and chest heaving. Then she collapsed, all the fight gone out of her. "Mom," she whispered, and began to weep.

CHAPTER 29

TEGAN HAD never spent a more miserable night.

On top of the devastating loss of Yanay, they were soaked and freezing with no wood to make a fire. Marcus was the only one who'd grabbed his pack in their panicked flight, leaving them with very little food or spare clothes. The rain ended as quickly as it began, but they were still trapped in the cramped cave with a ceiling so low they couldn't sit upright. Frequently, the frustrated spiders would stab their legs inside, trying to catch one of them with their claws. The group spent endless hours fending off the giant arachnids with their spears.

With the first pale light of dawn, the spiders disappeared. Exhausted, the group crawled from the cave and limped over to where the morning sun had begun to warm the rocks.

"Let's go after my mom," Ning croaked, her face haggard. None of them had slept.

Marcus stretched his back with grimace. "But we don't know where she is, or if she's still . . ." He trailed off awkwardly. "What I mean is, we need to talk this through before we start running through the woods calling her name."

Ning frowned and crossed her arms. "Okay, talk."

"Oh," Marcus said, looking uncomfortable from being put on the spot. "Well . . . the best way to find Yanay is to understand the spiders. That could help us figure out where they took her. We learned more about them last night."

"Like how they hang out on upturned tree roots," Tegan said. "That really happened, right?"

"Maybe it's a form of camouflage," Marcus said. "They're so big, they'd be seen if they were just sitting on the ground. By clinging to the bottoms of fallen trees, they blend in and their legs look like roots."

"Is that how they sleep or something?" Tegan asked.

"I guess so," Marcus said.

"We've seen a lot of weird-looking roots," Ning said with a shiver. "I hope they weren't all actually spiders."

"There are at least three," Tegan said. "The two that attacked our camp and the seven-eyed one that took Yanay."

"And think of all the eggs we've seen," Marcus

said. "Who knows how many of these things there are."

They fell silent as the terrifying reality sank in.

"If there's a lot of them, how can we ever find my mom?" Ning said. "She could be anywhere!"

Marcus began pacing. "Not all spiders are the same. Different types live in different ways."

"But these spiders are a whole new thing," Tegan said. "No one knows anything about them."

"Not necessarily," Marcus replied. "Remember I said they look like supersized huntsman spiders? Most spiders are loners, but huntsman spiders are one of the few social types. They live in large families, usually in some kind of den or nest."

Tegan frowned. "But the ones we've seen have been sleeping alone on fallen trees."

"Maybe they're the hunters or scouts, protecting the main nest," Marcus said.

"Is that where they would have taken my mom?" Ning asked.

Marcus shrugged. "It makes sense."

"Okay," Tegan said with a resigned sigh. "How do we find a monster lair?"

CHAPTER 30

"WE DON'T," Ed said.

They looked at him in surprise. He'd been so quiet, they'd almost forgotten he was there.

"But how else are we going to find Yanay?" Tegan asked.

Ed glanced at them before looking away. "We . . . we can't help her. We need to get out of here."

Tegan's face flushed as he stared at Ed in shock, his exhaustion and grief crumbling his inhibitions. "You coward," Tegan said, his fists clenched. "I always knew it. Mom would *never* give up on Yanay. She's the one who should have been on this trip. I hate that you're here. You're so embarrassing."

The words hit Ed like blows. He gazed at his son as his own face grew red. "Listen up. All of you. This will be hard to hear, but you need to face the facts. Yanay is probably dead. I'm sorry, Ning, I really am. I'm not trying to upset you. But we've all seen what *one* of those things can do, and now you want to go looking for a whole *nest* of them?" He thrust out his chin and shook his head. "No way. That's a death wish. We must be close to the trail by now, so we keep going south until we hit it. We'll find a ranger station, and they can organize a search party."

"But that could take days!" Ning cried. "She doesn't have that much time!"

Ed licked his lips and ran a trembling hand

through his thinning hair. "Maybe so, but I'm the adult here. I am not letting you go after her, and that's final."

"Adult?" Tegan said. "You're playing the adult card now? Well, how about *acting* like one? We saved *you* when you jumped off that cliff, remember? And during the spider attacks, you just sat there while Yanay and us *kids* did the fighting. Now you're claiming to be in charge? You make me sick. Go look for the trail, and we'll help Yanay. You're no use to us anyway!"

Ed stepped forward, towering over Tegan. He swayed silently, veins popping from his neck, before sticking a finger in Tegan's face. "You can't talk to me like that. I am your *father*! And that's hurtful, it really is."

"Hurtful?" Tegan said, his voice breaking. "You wanna talk about hurtful? How do you think I feel when you ignore me? I freaked out crossing that bridge, and where were you? Thinking about yourself, as always. We've been out here for nearly a week, lost, chased by monsters, almost dying, and you've never once asked me if I was okay. In case you're wondering, I'm not. I'm *terrified*. And really sad about Yanay. And worried I'll never see Mom again. But I can't even talk to you about that stuff, let alone expect you to help. How's that for *hurtful*?"

Ed looked down at Tegan for a long moment, his face now pale and drawn. His fists clenched and unclenched repeatedly. He started to speak, but stopped. Finally, he turned and walked a short distance away, where he stood staring into the forest.

Tegan glared at him, breathing hard, his heartbeat throbbing in his temples. Marcus and Ning sat nearby, wide-eyed.

After a few moments, Marcus asked, "Are you . . . okay?"

"Nope," Tegan said. "But that's not important right now." He took a deep, steadying breath. "Let's go find Yanay."

CHAPTER 31

"OKAY," MARCUS said. "Well, we know which way the spider went last night, so we can assume the lair is in that direction."

Tegan ran a hand through his tangled hair. "If there are as many of them as we think, and they live together, it would have to be someplace big, right?"

"But how could a place like that stay hidden?" Ning asked. "Wouldn't someone have noticed it by now?"

"Not if it's underground," came Ed's voice from behind them.

They turned in surprise to see Ed standing nearby, shifting his weight from one foot to the other.

"Mr. Campbell?" Ning said, the unspoken question in her eyes.

He took a step closer. "If you're all going, well . . . I'm going with you."

Ed briefly met Tegan's gaze before looking away. Tegan eyed him warily and swallowed the lump in his throat. If his dad could ignore what just happened, so could he. "Underground? Any idea where?"

"Maybe a cave," Ed said. "A deep one with multiple chambers that would fit them all. We could look for one with a big enough entrance."

Marcus nodded slowly. "We could follow the direction the spider went last night and search for caves in the cliffs along the way."

They grabbed their meager belongings and

headed into the trees. Ning took the lead, walking as quickly as the terrain allowed.

The hours crept by with agonizing slowness. As anxious as they were to find Yanay, their pace steadily decreased. The lack of food and sleep, along with the ongoing stress of being lost and hunted, had finally caught up with them. Their throats ached from calling Yanay's name. The blazing sun erased any trace of moisture from the previous night's brief storm. They doggedly scoured every cliff face, every slope for signs of a cave, but the few they found were too small. As the sun began to dip, so did their hopes.

Tegan tripped on a root and went down hard. He lay where he'd fallen, too exhausted to move.

Ed bent over with his hands on his knees, panting for breath. "You . . . okay?"

Through the pain, Tegan registered that his dad had actually shown some concern. He pushed himself up with a groan. "Having a hard time keeping my legs going."

Ning sat down heavily beside him. "Me too."

Marcus shuffled wearily over and pulled a bag of trail mix from his pack. "This is the last of it," he said as they each took a handful.

"Save a little for my mom," Ning said in a choked voice.

Marcus nodded with a sad smile.

"Sun's going down," Tegan said.

"We can't give up yet," Ning pleaded. "Please."

"No one's giving up," Ed said. "We'll keep going with flashlights if we have to."

Tegan glanced at him in surprise. His dad was acting differently since their fight.

They sat in silence, trying to find the strength to continue. A familiar shape at the base of a tree caught Tegan's eye. He stared at the gray egg, amazed that something so small could cause so much misery. Then he noticed another egg nearby. And a third.

"That's weird," Tegan said. "There are three eggs here."

"We normally only see one at a time," said Marcus.

Getting slowly to their feet, they followed the line of eggs to a small rise and labored up the slope. Ed gave a low whistle. "That's not something you see every day."

Scattered across a large clearing below them was a sea of spider eggs, half buried in the dirt. Hundreds of them. Their mottled gray surfaces shone dully in the fading light.

"It's a spider nursery," Marcus said in awe.

Ning grabbed Tegan's arm in a stone grip.

"Ow! What the—" he began, then stopped.

The far side of the egg-filled clearing ended at a cliff face. At the base of the cliff was the gaping maw of a giant cave.

CHAPTER 32

"IT LOOKS deep," Tegan said, staring intently at the cave opening.

"And it's right beside all these eggs," Marcus said. "This has to be it."

"Sun's almost down," Ed said. "They'll be awake."

Tegan narrowed his eyes at his father, but Ning spoke first. "We can't wait until morning. Think of what could be happening to her! We have to go in now!"

Ed put a shaky hand on Ning's shoulder, but his voice was steady. "I know."

"So for a plan," Marcus said, "maybe we could . . . um . . ."

Tegan's legs felt like marshmallows. "Rescue Yanay and don't die?"

Marcus shrugged. "I like it. A little light on specifics, but hey."

"We should make torches," Ning said.

"That will give us away," said Tegan.

"What's more important?" Marcus asked. "Stealth or protection?"

Ning hesitated. "If we have torches to start, we can always put them out later."

She sent them to get thick sticks while she quickly made a fire. Once the flames were going, Ning made multiple deep splits in one end of the sticks they'd found, using her pocket knife and a rock as a hammer. "Now jam strips of bark, chunks of wood, twigs, anything flammable you can find into the splits."

A few minutes later, they all stuck the bushy-looking ends of their sticks into the fire. The torches caught and burned brightly.

"Whoa, that's cool," Tegan said. "Where'd you learn how to do that?"

Ning's lip quivered. "My mom."

As they smothered the fire, the sun slipped behind the peak and twilight descended. Tegan gazed across the clearing at the cave. The pale eggs appeared ghostly in the gloom, like miniature tombstones in a graveyard. *That's appropriate,* Tegan thought. He glanced at the others—they looked like mourners at a funeral. With the unique twist that the funeral was their own. Torches held high, they headed down the slope.

A maze of roots covered the surface of the clearing. Tegan stepped onto them, carefully avoiding the eggs. The others moved to follow.

"Stop!" Tegan cried.

Ning froze, her foot raised above a root.

"I'm . . . stuck," Tegan said with a grunt. "My feet are glued to these roots. I can't move them!"

"It's like your sweatshirt," Ning said. "These roots must be covered with that same sticky stuff."

"We were right," said Marcus. "This isn't sap. The spiders coat tree roots with their webbing to make snares."

"It's how they protect all these eggs," Ning said. "Any predators would be trapped."

"Well, now *I'm* trapped," Tegan said, tugging on his legs. "And I can't . . . get . . . loose!"

"Looks like we'll have to cut off your feet," Ed said.

Aghast, Tegan turned to see his dad looking at him with a slight smile.

"Or you could take your boots off," Marcus said.

"Oh," Tegan said, his face flushed. "Right."

Untying his hiking boots, he carefully placed his sock-covered feet between the matrix of roots. The others followed him through the clearing. Avoiding both the eggs and the roots was like crossing a minefield.

Several minutes later, they stood before the entrance to the cave.

Tegan shivered. "Now the hard part."

CHAPTER 33

STEPPING INTO the cave was like plunging into a pool of ink. They moved slowly along the rocky floor, torches in one hand and spears in the other. Tegan wore his bow across his back, having stowed his few arrows in Marcus's pack along with their flashlights.

The cave narrowed to a large tunnel of rough stone that gradually sloped downward. There was no sign of the spiders.

"Is this the right place?" Marcus whispered.

"It has to be," Ning said with a catch in her voice. "It just does."

They shuffled forward, eyes straining to see past the dim light of their torches. Despite the chilly temperature, Tegan began to sweat. He felt as if they were walking down the throat of a giant beast.

Ning paused. "Do you hear that?" A steady hiss echoed out of the darkness.

"Is that . . . them?" Marcus asked, his eyes wide.

No one answered. Tegan's sense of dread grew with each passing moment. He dragged his boot-less feet forward, one reluctant step at a time. His socks were already torn, leaving his feet scraped and aching.

As the mysterious noise grew louder, so did the hammering of Tegan's heart. It took all his will-power to move blindly toward the eerie sound.

Every nerve in his body felt as taut as a violin string. By focusing hard on Yanay, he was able to keep going. Barely.

They caught a flicker of movement on the edge of the firelight. They thrust out their torches, spears at the ready. Nothing approached. No hideous form came hurtling out of the darkness.

Marcus shuffled tentatively forward. A cascading vertical surface shimmered and danced in the torchlight. With a sigh of relief, he lowered his spear. "It's a waterfall."

A sheet of water the width of the tunnel tumbled from a gap in the ceiling and entered a channel in the floor. The water flowed along the channel and disappeared through a hole in the wall. The way ahead was blocked.

Ning stamped her foot. "No! This *can't* be the end!"

"I'm really sorry, Ning," Ed said quietly.

She slid down the wall and sat with her head on her knees. Marcus stood nearby, his shoulders slumped. Tegan crouched beside Ning, wanting to comfort her, but not knowing how. He hoped simply being there was enough.

Spray from the fall tickled Tegan's face. Thinking the cold temperature might ease his aching feet, he stuck one foot into the falls to rest it on the rock behind the sheet of water.

His foot didn't hit anything. Puzzled, he stuck his spear into the falls, and it penetrated as far as he could reach. Lowering the tip, he felt it strike hard ground on the other side.

Marcus raised an eyebrow. "Do you think . . . ?"

Tegan stood and handed Marcus his torch. "Only one way to find out."

He took a deep breath and stepped through the waterfall.

CHAPTER 34

THE ICY blast took Tegan's breath away.

He emerged shivering on the far side. The muted glow of the torches shimmered indistinctly behind the curtain of water. Deeper into the cave, a dim green light shone in the distance.

Bracing himself, Tegan stepped back through the waterfall. "The c-cave . . . it k-keeps going," he said, his teeth chattering. "And there's some kind of glow on the other side."

Ning pulled him into a quick hug. "Thank you," she whispered.

"A glow?" Marcus asked. "From what?"

"Couldn't tell," Tegan said.

"The torches won't make it through the falls," Ed said. They dropped the flaming sticks, and Marcus dug the three flashlights from his pack. He passed two to Ning and Tegan. When he tried to give the last one to Ed, the man hesitated. "You keep it."

"Let's keep them off until we know what that glow is," Tegan said, sticking his flashlight in his back pocket. "If we link arms, the outer people can keep one hand on the tunnel walls to guide us."

They stepped through the waterfall and stood dripping and coughing on the other side. Linking arms, they shuffled slowly through the darkness toward the distant light.

Soon the glow resolved itself into oddly shaped

blotches on the walls and ceiling. Marcus approached the closest patch and touched it tentatively. "It's some kind of bioluminescent moss."

"Bioluma-what?" Tegan asked.

"Bioluminescent," Ning said. "A living thing that creates its own light."

The moss grew thicker as they walked, so they could move without flashlights. Eggs resting in niches in the rock walls and scatterings of stiff brown hairs confirmed that the spiders used this path. The tunnel gradually widened as it sloped downward. Around a nearby bend, the light seemed to increase, and they heard an odd clicking noise.

A wave of cold dread swept over Tegan, and he was seized by an urge to run screaming in horror.

Marcus trembled, casting anxious glances ahead of them. He looked ready to throw up. Ning put a hand on his shoulder. "I'm scared too," she said. "Why don't you stay here while I take a look?"

"I . . . I can't let you go alone," he stammered.

Tegan pointed to a horizontal crevice running through the rock wall, about two feet high. "That opening is too small for the spiders we've seen and runs in the same direction as the bend in the tunnel. Let's check it out."

Tegan wriggled into the crevice. Pulling out his flashlight, he cupped one hand over the end and clicked it on, allowing a bit of light to seep through his fingers as the others crowded in behind him.

As they crawled forward, the clicking noise grew louder. Soon a dull greenish glow appeared ahead of them, and Tegan turned off his flashlight. The crack angled upward, ending at a wide opening about three feet high. They quietly approached and looked through.

The sudden clench in Tegan's throat cut off his scream.

CHAPTER 35

THEY STARED down into a huge chamber. The glowing moss grew thickly, filling the space with an eerie green light. Stalactites hung from the high domed ceiling, while the walls were lined with numerous stone ledges.

And everywhere, crawling around and over each other, were the spiders. Monstrous, horse-sized spiders. Their multijointed legs looked like a forest of bent trees rippling in the wind. Tegan shook uncontrollably as the blood rushed from his head.

"No, no, no, no," Marcus whispered.

Ning gasped, her face ridged with terror as her eyes fixed on the near end of the chamber.

On a large shelf of rock sat a massive spider, three times larger than the rest. In contrast to its brown-haired companions, this one was grayish-white. Its twin rows of eyes were clouded, as if covered by a milky substance. The others swarmed nearby but never too close to the gray spider, which sat regally as if on a throne.

Pinned to the wall beside this monster was Yanay.

Her arms and legs were spread in an X shape with her wrists and ankles bound to the rock by thick webbing. Her skin looked ghastly pale, and she hung limply with her head slumped forward on her chest.

Tegan reached out and gripped Ning's hand.

The giant gray spider gave a series of loud chirps.

A knot of arachnids converged on a large spider and dragged it across the chamber floor, stopping below the rocky shelf on which the gray monster sat. The captured spider struggled furiously, while the rest of the horde rushed forward, chittering excitedly.

A moment later, the gray spider gave another sharp chirp. The spiders holding the prisoner fell upon it, fangs flashing and claws digging. In seconds, they tore it to shreds and began to feed.

Tegan watched in horror, his mouth frozen in a silent cry.

At a signal from Marcus, they retreated into the crevice and stared at each other in the faint glow of the chamber's moss.

"My *mom*," Ning whispered miserably, her face streaked with tears.

"We'll . . . we'll figure something out," Tegan said, but he had no idea how they could save Yanay. If she was even alive.

"It looks like she was given as a gift to the queen," Marcus said, his voice shaking.

"The big gray one is the queen?" Tegan asked.

"I think so," Marcus said.

"Why did they kill that one?" Ed asked, his eyes wide and his face streaked with sweat.

"It was probably a female," Marcus said. "The queen is usually the only reproductive spider in a cluster. Other females that are born into the group leave, or they're driven out. If they stay, then they're . . . eaten."

"But why?" Tegan asked.

"It's how the queen keeps her power," Marcus said. "She eliminates her rivals."

"My mom, is she . . . ?" Ning started to ask. Her voice cracked, and she squeezed her eyes shut, sending fresh tears coursing down her cheeks.

"I think she's alive," Marcus said hurriedly. "They wouldn't have bound her otherwise. She may have been bitten, though, and the venom could be why she looks . . . like that."

"Why is she stuck to the wall?" Tegan asked.

Marcus looked uncomfortable. "Um . . . I don't know. Not for sure, anyway."

"Tell me," Ning said fiercely. "What are you thinking?"

He hesitated for a long moment. "She could be a gift . . . of food."

CHAPTER 36

NING PLACED her head in the crook of her arm and sobbed.

Tegan put a hand on her shoulder and looked desperately at Marcus. "There must be *something* we can do!"

"Like what?" Marcus asked, wringing his hands. "There's a sea of monsters between us and Yanay!"

Tegan gripped his hair and turned hopefully

toward his dad. Ed ran a trembling hand over his stubbled beard and glanced toward the spiders' lair. He closed his eyes with a shiver and said nothing.

Tegan sighed, trying not to judge his father for being terrified when they all were. "I'm gonna look again."

He crawled back to the overlook, followed by Marcus and Ed. Cautiously, they pushed forward for a better view. Near the queen was the tunnel entrance. On the ground to one side, Tegan noticed an old backpack and the remains of a red flannel shirt. Apparently Yanay wasn't the first hiker the spiders had captured. The far end of the chamber was lost in deep shadow.

After a few minutes, they pulled back.

Marcus looked at Tegan. "Any ideas?"

"No. You?"

He shook his head miserably.

Ed glanced back the way they'd come. "Where's Ning?"

They scrambled down to where they'd left her.

Ning was gone.

Tegan's heart crumpled. *No! Not Ning!*

"None of the spiders can reach up this far, right?" Marcus asked anxiously.

With his heart in his mouth, Tegan moved quickly back to scan the chamber. It was the same horrifying scene, with no sign that Ning had been captured. Where could she have gone?

Ning appeared in the tunnel entrance near the queen and raised an object over her head.

Tegan gasped. A spider egg.

"Hey!" Ning shouted into the chamber. "Come and get me!" Holding the egg aloft, she fled back up the tunnel.

The queen gave a piercing shriek, and the mass

of spiders surged forward, clogging the tunnel entrance in their haste to pursue the egg thief.

"What is she *doing*?" Marcus exclaimed. "We have to help her!"

"But how?" Tegan asked.

They sat, paralyzed with indecision. The chamber was now empty save for the queen and Yanay.

"Did it work?" gasped a voice behind them.

Tegan spun to see Ning crawling toward them through the crevice. Relief washed over him. "Ning! What were you thinking?"

"Quick!" she said, heaving herself up to the overlook. "They'll figure out soon that I didn't go back down the tunnel. Hold my feet." Ning slid headfirst through the gap as Marcus and Tegan scrambled to grab her feet. Reaching down, she rested her palm on a narrow ledge and grasped the lip of the opening with her other hand. "Okay, let go."

Tentatively, they did as she asked. Ning carefully

lowered herself until she was crouching on the ledge about four feet below the overlook.

"There's a series of ledges almost all the way down," she whispered. "Come on, I'll guide you."

Tegan glanced at the queen, but her milky eyes were fixed on the tunnel, apparently unaware of the intruders high on the opposite wall. He looked over the edge, and his head spun. *I barely made it across the bridge,* Tegan thought. *How can I possibly do this?*

Then he remembered who had stayed with him on that bridge, believing in him, helping him face his fear. Yanay had been there when Tegan needed her.

And now she needed him.

"I gotcha," Ed said, grasping Tegan's hand. He caught his son's eyes and nodded. "You can do this."

Tegan looked awkwardly at his dad's earnest expression with a strange feeling of warmth. Taking a deep breath, he allowed Ed to slowly lower him over the edge. Ning caught his flailing feet, and soon he was perched on the ledge. Marcus, his breath coming in shallow gasps, came next, followed by Ed, who was tall enough to lower himself.

Ning led the way from ledge to ledge, making her way slowly down the wall. Tegan clung to the rock face, trying desperately not to look down. He focused on Ning's back, mimicking her movements, placing one quaking hand, then one shaky foot at a time. Bootless, he tried to grip the rock with his toes.

After several heart-stopping minutes, they reached the chamber floor. Tegan collapsed and tried not to throw up. They'd done it.

And then the queen began to shriek.

CHAPTER 37

"SHE'S WARNING the others!" Marcus said.

"Come on!" Ning called, and raced toward the queen's platform.

Tegan ran after her with his heart in his throat. They'd been forced to abandon their spears to make the treacherous climb down the chamber wall. The queen rose up like a terrifying cobra, her front legs extended with giant claws snapping.

Ning ran straight toward Yanay and pulled

herself onto the rocky shelf. The queen shrieked again and turned toward her.

Tegan grabbed a rock and hurled it at the massive spider. It struck her on the side of the head, causing her to pivot back toward them.

"Mom!" Ning cried, shaking Yanay's shoulders. "Mom, answer me!"

Yanay's eyes fluttered open. "Ning?" she croaked. "Is that really you?"

"I'm here," Ning replied through her tears.

Yanay's face took on a ghastly expression. "No! You have to get out of here. Leave me!"

"But I'm *saving* you!"

"You can't. I'm done. But you have a chance. *Run.*"

"No!" Ning said fiercely. "I won't leave you." She reached for the webs pinning Yanay to the rock.

"Don't touch them!" Marcus yelled. "You'll get stuck too!"

Tegan stood below the queen's rocky shelf,

thinking furiously. "Marcus, help Ning. Dad, we have to give them time by distracting the queen." As Marcus hurried toward Ning, Tegan threw another rock at the queen. It bounced off a hairy leg, earning him an angry hiss. Ed's rock struck her in the abdomen. She swung a gargantuan leg toward them, but the movement seemed sluggish. And surprisingly, she remained on her platform.

Tegan stared at the queen's graying body and rows of filmy eyes. "She's really old! If we can keep her away from Marcus and Ning, we might make it!"

As the queen turned back toward Yanay, Ed hit her with another rock, drawing her attention once again. Tegan snatched an old boot from the ground. It was unexpectedly heavy. He hurled it at the massive spider, trying not to think of what was inside.

"Better hurry!" Ed called. "We're running out of things to throw."

Marcus turned from tugging at Yanay's legs, his

eyes wild. "The webs are too strong! We can't touch them, and we can't break them!"

Tegan looked desperately around the cavern. There was nothing but the scattered remains of the dead spider—broken-off legs and the head, resting awkwardly on its twin fangs. *The fangs!* "Dad! Use one of these legs like a spear to distract the queen. Ning, I need your help!"

Gingerly, Ed picked up one of the dead spider's legs, his face wrinkled in disgust. Struggling with the awkward appendage, he approached the queen and jabbed the clawed end at the monster, who turned to face him.

Ning appeared beside Tegan as he kicked at one of the dead spider's fangs. "Help me break them off!"

"Hurry!" Marcus cried. "The others will be back soon!"

Tegan and Ning kicked frantically at the thick

fangs. Every blow sent a fresh wave of pain through Tegan's bare foot.

"They won't break!" Ning cried in frustration.

"Bring the whole head!" Marcus yelled.

They bent down on either side of the dead spider's giant head. Tegan's stomach churned as his hands touched the hairy exoskeleton. Grimacing, he turned his face away, trying not to stare into the creature's many vacant eyes.

They lifted the heavy head and staggered over to Marcus, who helped them haul it onto the rocky shelf. While Ed kept the queen's attention, Ning and Tegan scrambled up and heaved the head toward Yanay.

"Leave me," she said weakly. "There's no time."

Ignoring her, they maneuvered the head so the edge of a fang rested against the webbing around Yanay's right hand and began an awkward sawing motion.

"It's . . . working!" Tegan said, grunting with effort.

Soon the webbing split. "Mom, pull!" Ning cried. Yanay strained against the bonds, her jaw clenched. A moment later, her hand broke free from the sticky substance.

As they shifted the head down to Yanay's ankle, Tegan glanced over at his dad. Exhausted, his face haggard, Ed doggedly pressed the attack on the frustrated queen. Despite their terrifying situation, Tegan noticed an unfamiliar feeling as he watched his father—pride.

They soon had Yanay's remaining limbs free. She collapsed against Ning, who lowered her gently to the ground. Yanay gazed up at her daughter, her glazed eyes brimming with tears. "I love you," she whispered.

"Love you too, Mom," Ning said in a choked voice.

"Time to go," Marcus said. "*Now.*"

They helped Yanay off the platform. Tegan turned to call his dad, but when he saw the tunnel entrance, the words died in his throat.

The spiders had returned.

CHAPTER 38

THEIR ONLY escape route was overflowing
with monsters.

"Run!" Marcus yelled.

Ed dropped the heavy spider leg and staggered
after the others toward the far end of the chamber.
Tegan looked desperately for another way out but
saw only solid stone walls. Ahead, a forest of narrow stalagmites rose from the cavern floor. Beyond
it, the chamber was draped in darkness.

Yanay stumbled between Marcus and Ning,

rousing slowly from the effects of the venom. The spiders raced after them, covering the distance with frightening speed.

Tegan reached the darkness and plunged ahead.

"Gah!" he cried as he stepped into frigid water. His eyes adjusted, revealing a large pool completely covering the end of the chamber. Across the water towered a blank stone wall. There was no way out.

The group turned and faced the monsters. The spiders slowed in anticipation, chirping excitedly by rubbing their front appendages against their jaws.

Trapped between a horde of monsters and the icy water, Tegan found himself picturing things he'd never see again—his cat, Buford, asleep on the quilt his grandma had made. His mom trying not to smile as he batted his eyes when he was in trouble. He thought of experiences he'd never have, like driving his aunt Jackie's 1974 Mustang or kissing Megan Franklin or working at the Sugarbowl.

A burning sensation flamed in Tegan's chest, roaring in strength until his anger consumed his fear. No, not anger. *Fury.* He clenched his fists. If this was the end, he would go out fighting.

Tegan picked up a rock and hurled it at the nearest spider. His throw went wide, and the stone smacked into a stalagmite. The narrow pillar snapped off, leaving a jagged point. His mind whirled. Turning to the others, he called, "Break off the stalagmites! Make spears!"

Tegan raced forward and picked up the fallen rock. He struck the base of a pillar, which broke free, forming a crude stone spear. The others hurried to follow his example. Ed turned toward the water to search for a rock, but hesitated and looked intently into the pool. A moment later, he dove headfirst into the water and disappeared.

"Dad!" Tegan cried. "Come back!"

The ripples in the pool quickly faded. Ed didn't resurface.

The remaining group huddled together, holding their makeshift weapons. Yanay stood by sheer force of will, her expression radiating fierce determination. The spiders pressed closer and reached toward them with cruel claws.

Tegan wavered unsteadily. Ed's abandonment had snuffed out his anger, leaving him weak and hollow. *I'm so tired of being afraid,* he thought.

He closed his eyes and braced himself for the final blow.

CHAPTER 39

A SPLASH disturbed the surface of the water.

Tegan whirled to see his dad floating in the pool.

"Follow . . . m-m-me," Ed said, his teeth chattering. "B-big breath." He turned and dove.

Ning hurled her stalagmite at an approaching spider before helping her mom into the pool. The water seemed to revive Yanay, and she pulled her arm from her daughter's grasp. "I can swim."

Marcus and Tegan quickly followed, whimpering when the cold water reached their waists. Together, they took deep breaths and plunged beneath the surface.

Tegan opened his eyes and panicked in the inky darkness. It was as if a sea monster had swallowed him whole. But soon his eyes adjusted. Ning was beside him, and in the distance, he spied a hint of movement that must be his dad. Tegan swam desperately after him.

A pale circle of light appeared. As Tegan approached, he realized the glow came from an underwater hole in the rock wall. Ed disappeared inside, followed by the others. Already feeling the need to breathe, Tegan entered the opening.

They swam through a dim passage. Tegan struggled to pull himself through the water. His clothes were like anchors dragging him down. He fought to hold his breath, but bubbles exploded from his lips. Spots of light danced in his vision, and his lungs felt crushed in a vise. He panicked, thrashing wildly in the confined space.

Finally, he spotted the surface, and thrust upward. Suddenly air, glorious air, surrounded his head. Tegan sucked in a ragged breath, thinking nothing in his life had ever felt so wonderful. For a long moment, he thought only of the sweet sensation of air filling his lungs.

When his breathing slowed, Tegan saw that everyone had surfaced. They were floating in a small cave pool. Ahead of them, the water flowed from the entrance and joined a wide, calm river. His limbs leaden, he swam slowly after the others, emerging from the cave into the bright light of the full moon.

They dragged themselves onto a rocky shoreline

and collapsed. Soon Tegan crawled to where Ning hovered over Yanay.

"Is she . . . all right?" he asked.

A faint smile crossed Yanay's lips. "I've been better," she said weakly. "But thanks to you all, I'm alive to feel this terrible."

Ning broke into a crying laugh and hugged her mom. Ed sat heavily beside Tegan, and they stared at each other in stunned silence.

Finally, Ed said, "I can't believe we made it out of there."

"Thanks to you," Tegan said.

He gave a tired chuckle. "I told you I was a good swimmer."

Tegan remembered the warmth he'd felt when Ed helped him down the chamber wall, and his sense of pride while watching his dad distract the queen.

"I'm . . . I'm glad you came with us," Tegan said awkwardly.

Ed's face lit up for a moment, but then his smile faded. "I heard what you said. You know . . . earlier. I didn't like it, but I heard it. I'll . . . try to do better. To *be* better. And you can always talk to me about anything, okay?"

A lump swelled in Tegan's throat. Not trusting himself to speak, he nodded.

"Listen, I know you wanted Mom on this trip and got stuck with me," Ed continued. "But when her work conflict came up, I was actually glad."

"You were?" Tegan asked in surprise. "Why?"

"Because, well . . . I know I haven't been the best father. I want to change that. To spend more time with you."

Tears pricked Tegan's eyes. "You always hang out with just Milo. I . . . I thought you didn't like me."

Ed grimaced. "Of course I do. When you were

born, I was young and felt so . . . inadequate. I screwed up a lot. I was able to fix some of those mistakes with Milo, and I wanted to come on this trip to fix things with you. I know I've made a mess of that, but I want to keep trying . . . if it isn't too late."

Tegan's mind reeled as he gazed at his father's hopeful expression. "It's not too late."

Ed pulled Tegan into a rough hug. Things were still broken between them, but now Tegan believed they could be mended.

With Ning's help, Yanay sat up. "The only river this big around here flows through Shadow Canyon."

Marcus looked at her sharply, his eyes bright with excitement. "So we can follow it to the bridge!"

Yanay nodded, and they all gave a ragged cheer.

Tegan slumped in relief, resting his forehead on his knees. They were going to make it. He would see his mom's crooked smile again. Enjoy the sweet scent on Buford after he hunted in the lilac bushes. Snuggle under the blue quilt his grandma made him for Christmas. He was going home.

Tegan raised his head for a grateful look at the star-filled sky. Only minutes ago, he thought he'd never see it again. He glanced back at the cave.

Pouring from the walls of the entrance came the spiders.

CHAPTER 40

ONE SPIDER after another emerged from the cave, swarming across the cliff face toward the riverbank.

"Run!" Tegan yelled.

The group's confused expressions turned to horror. Staggering up, they stumbled across the rocky beach and plunged blindly into the forest. A branch slapped Tegan in the face, cutting his cheek. He raised his arms protectively and kept going.

"Follow the river to the bridge!" Yanay called.

Tegan heard the spiders crashing through the brush behind them. Still running, Marcus pulled off his waterlogged pack and dug out the flashlights. He passed two to Ning and Yanay, keeping the third for himself.

Twin beams cut the darkness, allowing them to increase their speed.

"Mine's dead!" Yanay said, banging the flashlight against her palm before tossing it aside.

The sounds of pursuit were now coming from both sides as the spiders closed in. Tegan's legs dragged, and it felt like a python was squeezing his chest. His bare feet slammed painfully onto sticks and rocks. And spreading through him like a poison was the sickening realization that they would lose this race.

They burst into a wide moonlit meadow. In the center stood a rock the size of a small bus, dotted with moss and scattered debris. As they raced across the open ground, the spiders entered the clearing. Without the trees to slow them, they scuttled forward, legs churning with sickening speed. They would be on the group in moments.

"Climb the rock!" Ning gasped.

She scrambled up the smooth, curving surface, finding small indents invisible to Tegan. Reaching back, Ning helped the others claw their way to the top, where they collapsed, chests heaving.

Tegan looked back, his blood chilling. The spiders had them completely surrounded. They were on a stone island in a sea of monsters. There was no escape.

The spiders formed a thick ring around the stone, darting forward, but always pulling back just before they reached it.

"They're not climbing after us," Ning said in confusion.

Yanay shook her head. "It's like they're hesitant to touch the rock."

"How did they come after us so fast?" Ed asked in frustration. "There's no way they could swim through that narrow tunnel."

"They must have another way out," Marcus said.

The stone trembled slightly beneath them. Tegan's eyes widened. "Please tell me I imagined that."

"Earthquake?" Ning asked.

Marcus stared intently at the spiders, then down at the rock. He bent over and touched the stone, rapping it with his knuckles. "Um . . . I don't think this is a rock."

Tegan looked at his friend like he'd lost his mind. "What are you talking about? If it's not a rock . . ." Realization hit as he glanced down at the dappled gray surface. Unusually smooth. Roughly oval shaped. "It can't be," he whispered in disbelief.

Another tremor shook their island. "It's an egg," Marcus said.

"But why is it so huge?" Ning asked.

"It must be a queen's egg!" Marcus said. "The queen back in the lair is really old. That's why she couldn't fight very well. This must be the oversized egg of the new queen, the one that will replace her when she dies."

"That's why the spiders aren't attacking us," Tegan said. "They don't want to risk damaging the egg."

"So we're safe," Ning said. "We can wait here until morning when the spiders go back to their lair!"

Marcus examined the surface of the egg. "We may not have that long. Our climbing up here probably bothered her. I think she's hatching."

As if the giant baby spider heard him, a long crack appeared beneath their feet.

"We *cannot* catch a break!" Tegan growled.

"What happens when the new queen hatches?" Ning asked.

Marcus gazed mournfully at them, his face ghostly in the moonlight. "She'll need to feed."

CHAPTER 41

"AND WE'RE breakfast," Tegan said, his heart dropping like a stone.

He slumped down, surrendering to hopelessness. Lying back, he looked up at the ocean of stars. *It really is beautiful,* he thought numbly. *Not a bad last view.* Tegan shifted uncomfortably, his bow digging into his shoulder. He'd grown so used to carrying it across his back that he'd almost forgotten it was there.

He sucked in a sharp breath and sat up quickly. "Ning, can you make a fire?"

Her face wrinkled in confusion. "I have my flint, but there's hardly anything to burn up here. It's not like we could make a bonfire and fight them off."

"I don't need a bonfire, only a little flame," Tegan said.

The egg shifted again. New cracks emerged, and the split below them grew wider.

"Grab everything you can find," Ning said as she dug in her pocket for the flint.

They spread out across the surface of the egg and brought back dried moss, a few leaves, and some twigs.

"You'd better be ready," Ning said to Tegan. "If I can get this started at all, it's going to go fast."

He pulled the bow off his back. "Marcus, pass me the arrows."

Marcus's eyes widened as he grasped Tegan's plan. He quickly tore open his pack and reached inside. His shoulders slumped. He held up the three arrows—two were snapped in half, their tips hanging limply. "Only one left."

Tegan swallowed hard as he carefully took the last arrow. "I need something to make the tip burn."

"You can use some of this dried moss," Ning said. "But I don't know how you'll get it to stick."

Tegan looked around desperately. There was nothing here, nothing but a cracking egg.

Then he realized that might be just what he needed.

Taking the arrow, Tegan plunged the tip through the crack into the yellow-green yolk. It came away coated with the slime. He wiped off the excess on the edge of the shell and pressed a handful of moss to the tip. It stuck with surprising firmness.

He looked at Ning. "Ready."

She struck the flint, sending a spark into the small pile of debris.

Nothing happened.

She tried again, then a third time with the same result. The next tremor hit, so strong it sent Marcus stumbling toward the slope of the egg, his arms flailing helplessly. Ed leaped forward and caught his wrist just before Marcus fell over the side.

Tegan turned back to Ning. "No pressure or anything, but we're all about to die."

"Not. Helpful," she growled between strikes of the flint. Ning dropped her face to the pile and blew gently. A spark had caught, but would it light? "Come on," she muttered between breaths.

A small flame sprang up, curling the leaves and catching the tiny tent of twigs.

"Hurry!" Ning cried.

Already the newborn flame was dying. Tegan

thrust the arrow's moss-covered tip into the fire. The flames licked greedily at the dry moss.

He tried to nock the arrow onto the string, but his shaking hand kept missing. The egg gave another violent tremor, forcing him to catch his balance.

"Tegan . . ." Ning warned.

The arrow finally found the string. Tegan drew back and raised his hand to his cheek. He sighted on the nearest spider, a huge brown one with black streaks, chittering excitedly in a large pack.

Tegan hesitated. Each missed practice shot replayed in his mind with excruciating clarity. He heard the echo of his father's laughter at every failure. *What am I thinking? I only have one shot. I can't do this.*

A voice sounded close to his ear, soft and low. "You've got this, son."

"Shoot!" Marcus yelled.

CHAPTER 42

THE ARROW arced through the air, tracing a line of fire across the night. The single-second flight seemed to take an hour. Tegan held his breath.

The flaming tip buried itself in the spider's side.

The monster shrieked, rearing up on its back legs. The flames licked quickly across its hairy exoskeleton. The spider crashed down onto the one beside it, thrashing wildly. The second spider began to burn and blundered into a third.

The nearby spiders tried to pull back, but they

were pinned by the eager press of those behind them. The three flaming spiders raced through and over the crowd, lighting others as they went. The fire spread across the monsters until they all began fleeing in panic.

"Yes!" Ning cried, and wrapped Tegan in a bear hug.

He felt a hand on his shoulder and turned to see his dad beaming down at him, tears in his eyes. As the meadow emptied of spiders, the lump in Tegan's throat swelled, choking off any words. But his smile said enough.

And then the egg split in two.

They were thrown airborne, tumbling through the night. Ning cried out in pain, and Marcus crashed into a pile of brush. Tegan landed on his back, and his breath flew out in a whoosh, leaving him gasping like a dying fish. After fifteen agonizing seconds, he sucked in a small breath. Soon the iron grip on his chest relaxed, and he breathed normally again.

Marcus pulled him to his feet as the others ran over. Ed limped slightly.

"You okay?" Tegan choked out to his dad.

"Just a sprain. Ning got the worst of it."

Ning cradled one arm and leaned on Yanay. She grimaced and said, "Don't think I'll be climbing for a while."

From between the broken halves of the egg, a gargantuan shape heaved up. Covered in slime, the new queen spread her cramped legs. One clawed foot struck the ground beside them, driving into the earth like a spike.

"This way!" Yanay yelled and began stumbling across the now vacant clearing. Tegan threw his dad's arm over his shoulder and followed.

Behind them, an unearthly shriek ripped the

night. The ground shook as if pounded by a giant's fist. The queen was giving chase.

They raced into the woods at the far edge of the meadow. Moments later, Tegan heard limbs cracking and a frustrated screech.

"She's too big!" Marcus panted. "Can't fit between the trees."

They ran for several minutes as the queen's cries grew fainter behind them. Finally, they staggered to a halt. The moonlit forest was blessedly quiet. The only sounds were their labored breathing and the rushing river in the nearby ravine.

"Everyone okay?" Yanay asked. "Other than Ning's arm and Ed's ankle, that is."

Tegan nodded, too exhausted to speak.

"What about you?" Marcus wheezed.

"The venom's wearing off," Yanay said. "The cold water and running helped."

"We should keep going," Ning said. "They could start chasing us again."

Tegan wanted to collapse, but knew Ning was right. A strange noise caught his attention. "Do you hear that?"

Out of the darkness behind them came a thrashing sound, growing rapidly closer.

"They're coming!" Marcus said.

"No, listen." Tegan had heard spiders racing through the forest before. This was something else.

A creature burst from the shadows and was on them before they could move. A hulking shape with spikes on its head flashed by them and disappeared.

"Was that an elk?" Marcus asked in disbelief.

Another animal, long and low with a thick tail, whipped past in near silence.

"Mountain lion," Yanay said.

Was it chasing the elk? Tegan wondered.

Next came a fox, a pair of wolves, and finally a huge, lumbering bear. The animals ignored them and each other, racing away into the night.

"What is going on?" Ed demanded.

On the wind came a familiar scent—smoke. Behind them in the dark woods, pinpricks of orange light sprang up. They grew larger and connected into a wavering line.

Realization hit Tegan like a baseball bat as he remembered Yanay's constant warnings about their campfires. The burning spiders had gone into the dry trees, igniting a forest fire.

Tegan groaned. They were being chased again—this time by flames.

CHAPTER 43

"RUN!" YANAY yelled.

They turned and fled after the animals. The safety of the river was far below them in the dark ravine. It was too dangerous to jump into the swirling, rock-filled water now. Their only hope was reaching the bridge.

Pushing through a wall of brush, they found themselves back on the elusive trail they'd left almost a week ago, but there was no time to celebrate. They ran wearily in the moonlight, retracing their steps. Behind them, Tegan heard the snap and pop of trees splintering from the intense heat.

Their injuries and the uphill grade slowed their pace. The wave of heat grew behind them, pushing them forward. Driven by a strong wind, the fire surged past on either side as they struggled up the steep trail.

Tegan sucked in hot air and began to choke. His eyes itched and burned from the billowing smoke. He caught a glimpse of Ning's soot-stained face, her expression reflecting his own fear, helplessness, and frustration. Had they survived everything they'd been through only to die in a forest fire?

"There!" Ed shouted.

Through the trees and swirling ash, they spied the bridge.

Everyone shot forward in a burst of adrenaline-fueled speed. They were going to make it.

Rounding the curve of the trail, they rushed to

the bridge entrance and slid to a stop. There hung the matching pairs of thick support cables, securely anchored to the far side. But between them, the walkway's wooden planks were burned and charred, some hanging loosely, others missing completely. The fire had gotten there first.

"No!" Marcus wailed. Holding on to a nearby sapling, he tentatively placed one foot on the nearest smoking plank. It snapped beneath his weight.

Tegan gripped his ash-covered hair and stared longingly at the far side of the canyon, free of the raging flames. It was only a hundred feet away, but it might as well have been a hundred miles.

The fire pushed closer, hemming them in from all sides. They huddled together in a small clearing near the bridge. Ning examined the cables and shouted over the roar of the flames. "They look solid! I think we can make it!"

"What?" Tegan cried, realizing what she was proposing. "I can't do that!"

"Yes, you *can*." Ning touched the top cable and yanked her hand back. "Hot! Wrap your hands in something!"

Marcus threw his backpack to the ground and pulled out a spare shirt. Tearing off one of the sleeves for himself, he tossed the remainder to Tegan and Ed.

"We'll go together," Yanay said to Ning. Using strips of cloth from her shirt, she wrapped Ning's good hand, then her own. Gripping the waist-high support cable, Ning put her foot on the lower cable that previously held the walkway. Moving gingerly, she stepped out into the void. The cables swung erratically for a moment, but she steadied herself. Yanay moved quickly behind her, ready to help Ning as she shifted forward using only one hand.

"Marcus, go!" Ed yelled. "Take the other side!"

Marcus, his eyes hidden by the flames reflected in his glasses, hurried to the opposite edge of the bridge. Placing his wrapped hands on the top cable, he stepped out and was soon moving steadily across.

Tegan finished wrapping his torn feet and turned to his dad, tears streaming down his face. "I don't think I can do this!"

Ed took Tegan's shoulders and spoke over the roar of the flames. "You've done incredible things out here, son. You're strong and brave, way braver than me. I'll be right beside you. Let's go home."

Confidence swelled inside of Tegan, stronger than his terror. The fear still hovered like a phantom, but it no longer paralyzed him.

Tegan approached the bridge. He gripped the top cable tightly to stop his hands from shaking. The heat from the braided metal seeped through the cloth. He swallowed hard and took a deep breath.

Then Tegan stepped out into space.

CHAPTER 44

THEY WERE quiet on the ride home, each needing to be alone with their thoughts.

Ed navigated as Yanay drove the winding forest roads. Tegan and Ning sat behind them while Marcus curled up in the SUV's back row.

At a campground, Yanay wrapped Ed's ankle and made a sling for Ning's arm, then washed and bandaged the cuts on Tegan's feet. Ed found a forest ranger and reported the fire. Fearing what people might think, they decided to not mention the spiders, at least for now.

At a gas station, they gorged on hot dogs and candy, which brightened their mood. Back on the highway, Tegan noticed a billboard advertising the spooky Grimstone Manor ride at ThrillVille amusement park. He shook his head—he'd had enough spookiness for the rest of his life.

"Hey, Marcus," Ed said. "I think you should be the one to name that spider species. It'd look great on your college applications for zoology."

"Yeah," Ning said. "You could call them *Biggus horrificus*."

"Or *Arachnis t-rexicus*," Marcus said.

Their laughter began to melt the lingering tension. To Tegan, if felt like they were celebrating being alive. He allowed himself a smile.

The nightmare was finally over.

EPILOGUE

MARCUS LAY sprawled on his bed, soaking in the comfort of being home. He gazed at the animal classifications poster on his wall and the glow-in-the-dark constellations stuck to the ceiling. While listening to the gentle gurgle of his fish tank, he savored the smell of worn socks, old pizza, and sweet chili Doritos. A few days ago, he thought he'd never see this place again.

Rousing himself, Marcus hopped off the bed and emptied his backpack. He carefully laid the items he'd collected from the forest on his desk—three pine cones, leaves from five different tree species, an abandoned bird's nest, a mouse skull, an owl feather, and finally, an egg the size of a swollen football with an unusual gray-patterned shell.

He lovingly stroked the egg, picturing his display for the school science fair this fall . . . and the blue ribbon attached to it. "I'm going to have the best science exhibit ever!"

"Marcus?" called a voice from downstairs. "Dinner!"

"Coming, Mom!" He hurried out of the room and closed the door behind him.

A few moments later, the egg trembled and began to crack.

ACKNOWLEDGMENTS

ACKNOWLEDGMENTS ARE tricky. While only my name is on the cover, putting a Monsterious book into the world takes an entire team of talented, dedicated people at home, at my literacy agency, and at my publisher. Then another army of book lovers steps up to help it find its way into the hands of readers—reviewers, booksellers, teachers, librarians, fellow authors, friends, and fans.

There is no way to thank you all properly, so I will simply say this—from my twelve-year-old self, who dreamed of my stories one day entertaining and inspiring people, and my awestruck present self, desperately hoping I don't wake up from this dream, I give you my deepest thanks.

In the Special Mentions section, a huge thank-you goes to my talented and generous author wife,

Lisa McMann; my ever-supportive grown-up kids, Kilian and Kennedy; my steadfast agent, Michael Bourret; my fearless publisher, Jennifer Klonsky; my incredible editors, Stephanie Pitts and Matt Phipps; and the wonderful Ryan Quickfall, whose eye-grabbing art adorns each Monsterious cover.

Finally, to all my readers—these books would not exist without you. I sincerely hope they give you the joy I've always found in books. Your enthusiasm, excitement, encouragement, and support give this Monsterious series a claw-footed foundation on which to stand and leathery wings with which to fly. On to the next adventure!

Photo © Kennedy McMann

As a professional musician, **Matt McMann** played an NFL stadium, a cruise ship, and the International Twins Convention. Now he writes the kind of spooky mystery-adventure books he loved as a kid. He's hiked the Pacific Northwest, cruised Loch Ness, and chased a ghost on a mountain. While he missed Bigfoot and Nessie, he caught the ghost. He enjoys brainstorming new books with his wife, *New York Times* bestselling author Lisa McMann; viewing his son Kilian McMann's artwork; and watching his daughter, actor Kennedy McMann, on television.

You can visit Matt at
MattMcMann.com

And follow him on Instagram and Twitter
@Matt_McMann

LOOK OUT FOR MORE THRILLS AND CHILLS IN THE MONSTERIOUS SERIES!

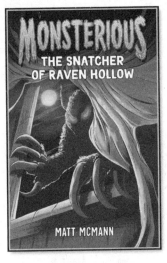